THE LONG, HARD RIDE

Bolt had been in the saddle since the rainy dawn, and most of the ride had been hard, filled with frustration and fear.

Now, working one shoulder at a time, Loretta massaged Bolt's flesh briskly to return the warmth to his body. And Bolt could feel the tension leaving his legs as she boldly continued to work with her hands.

"Relax," Loretta urged. "Your muscles are so hard I can't even massage them!"

Bolt concentrated on loosening up, but parts of his body became even more stiff.

"Roll over on your back," Loretta ordered, "and I'll warm up your front."

Bolt rolled over and pulled Loretta's soft body to his.

"I'm already so hot, I'm about to boil over," he husked. "Now, how about my warming you up?"

Loretta grinned at Bolt's suggestion. "You just finished one long, hard ride. Are you sure you're ready for another?"

BOLT #8

HARD IN THE SADDLE

BY CORT MARTIN

ZEBRA BOOKS
KENSINGTON PUBLISHING CORP.

ZEBRA BOOKS

are published by

KENSINGTON PUBLISHING CORP.
475 Park Avenue South
New York, N.Y. 10016

Printed in the United States of America

Chapter One

A hush fell over the back corner of the Red River Saloon as the onlookers watched Bolt intently to see if he would play his hand on out against the Major. A lot of money was riding on his decision. The other three players in the poker game had already folded, pushed their cards toward the center of the table.

Bolt glanced at the pile of poker chips that had accumulated in the pot during this one hand, then over at the neat stack of chips in front of Major Farrington. If Bolt called the Major, it would take all of his own remaining chips to see the man's hand. If he lost, he would be down over five hundred dollars for the night. But if he won, he would rake in a healthy stash. He figured there was almost twelve hundred dollars in the kitty and the Major had just raised again, forcing the other players to fold.

The next move was up to Bolt.

Since he joined the poker game some three hours ago, he had watched the other players closely, looking for the telltale signs that would indicate if they had winning hands or were bluffing their way through. It had been easy to spot the conspicuous gestures of two of the players. One of them was just a scrawny kid named Frank who couldn't manage to suppress a smile whenever he got the good cards. Bolt could read the body movement of the man on his left as well. Perkins, a tall, thin man who looked like a drifter, had a habit of sitting up tall in his chair and leaning forward when he liked the cards he drew. He also wore a frown on his face when he had a good hand, as if to fool the others. It was when he leaned back in his chair, a smug look on his face, that Bolt knew he was bluffing. It had taken Bolt a little longer to figure out Vic Butler's telltale gesture. The heavy man kept a poker face, but when he drew a winning hand, he gripped his right wrist with his left hand for a brief moment, as if to keep anyone from taking the cards away from him.

Bolt studied Farrington's face, trying to determine if the man was bluffing. He had called Bolt, raised him another hundred. The Major was a distinguished looking man, with neatly trimmed gray hair, crystal clear blue eyes. He wore neat brown trousers, a long-sleeved white shirt. An hour ago, he had removed his matching brown jacket, rolled his shirt sleeves up. He smoked a pipe, but most of the time the pipe sat in an ashtray, unlit. When Bolt looked into Farrington's sparkling blue eyes, he saw that the elderly gentleman was staring at him, waiting patiently for Bolt to make his move.

It was unnerving to have all of the eyes of the other players and the bystanders focused on him. The muscles in Bolt's stomach quivered and tightened, but on the outside, he appeared cool and calm. So did Farrington.

The beautiful owner of the Red River Saloon, Amylou Lovett, had been absolutely correct about the Major. He was a damned good poker player. When Bolt had asked Miss Lovett if there were any decent players in town, she had nodded her head toward the back corner table.

"Major Daniel Farrington, over there, is the best player in Houston," she had said. "Best in the whole west, probably."

6

"Is he honest?" Bolt had asked.

"Straight as an arrow." The tall, slender, dark-haired beauty had told Bolt that the gray-haired man was a retired Major from the Confederate Army who spent all of his time playing poker in various parts of Texas, looking for someone who was good enough to beat him.

That was all Bolt wanted to know. He had quite a reputation himself as a poker player. It would be a fair match.

"Don't play against the Major unless you can afford to lose," she had warned, smiling with red, wet, sensuous lips, batting her eyes flirtatiously.

"Don't worry about me." Bolt had returned her smile. "I hadn't planned to."

But Amylou Lovett was one of the people watching Bolt now as he weighed his chances of winning the pot.

Bolt didn't need to look at the cards in his hand again for reassurance. He knew what he had. The best hand he'd had all night. Two pair, aces over jacks. There were other combinations that could beat it, but did the Major hold one of them? Farrington had successfully bluffed him a couple of times before, so there was no way of knowing if he was trying to sucker him in again. That was what Bolt liked about the game. The challenge of playing against an expert.

Keeping his eyes locked on Farrington's, Bolt pushed his remaining chips into the pot.

"I'll see you, Major."

Dan Farrington placed his cards on the table, fanned them out so Bolt could see them. Miss Lovett and the men grouped around the table edged in closer to see his hand, waited for Bolt to show his cards.

But Bolt didn't display his cards. Instead, he cursed under his breath as he looked at the four tens and a five spot that were spread out in front of Farrington.

"The pot's yours," Bolt said without emotion as he folded his cards, placed them face down on the table and pushed them into the other discarded cards.

The onlookers gasped, then began congratulating the Major. Bolt looked up at Amylou Lovett. She smiled and shrugged her shoulders as if to say, "I told you so." Her smile was disarming and her dark eyes danced playfully as she looked over at Farrington and back to Bolt. She was challenging him to keep the game going.

"You're not going to show your cards?" Farrington asked, a trace of a smile on his lips.

"Nope. You'll never know if I was bluffing or not."

"I like that, Bolt. You're a damned good player. Best I've run across in quite a spell." He scooped in the chips from the center of the table, began arranging them in neat stacks. "Everybody still in the game?" He looked around at the other players.

"Not me, Major," said Perkins. His chair scraped across the floor as he stood up and left the table.

"I've had enough for tonight," said Vic Butler. He stood up and was joined by young Frank, who just shook his head.

"Looks like it's just the two of us," said the Major, "unless you're ready to pack it in."

Bolt glanced up at Miss Lovett again, was charmed by her encouraging smile. He was out of chips, but he still had a thousand dollars with him, ten hundred-dollar bills stashed in his wallet. He fished the wallet out of his pocket, drew out the bills.

"You got more chips, Miss Lovett?"

"No need to get chips," said Farrington. "With just

8

the two of us, we can use cash, if that's all right with you."

"Fine by me."

"One more hand. Winner take all. And to make it more interesting, I'll fatten the kitty with all the chips before we start. He pushed the chips into the center of the table. "Ante up. A hundred-dollar ante, hundred-dollar bets?" He counted out ten bills from his money-clip, put the rest of his money away, then looked up to see if Bolt approved of the new rules.

Bolt slid a hundred-dollar bill into the chips in the middle of the table. Farrington matched the ante with his own bill.

Amylou Lovett stepped forward, raised her hand.

"Just a minute, gentlemen. I'd like to buy you both a drink for luck. Carl, bring two glasses of whiskey over here."

Farrington left the cards on the table until Carl Anders, the bartender, had delivered the drinks. Carl was a thin man with blonde hair. He was tightlipped, cold as mutton, as he set the drinks down without smiling.

Bolt and the Major each took a polite sip of the whiskey, nodded to Miss Lovett, then set the drinks aside.

Farrington gathered up the cards, shuffled them, then pushed them across the table for Bolt to cut. Bolt took a few cards off the top, set them next to the big stack, then placed the others on top of them. When the elderly man was through dealing, Bolt picked up his cards and looked at them. Not a very good start. A king and ten of hearts, and three low cards, all of different suits.

Bolt watched as Farrington picked up his cards and

studied them. The Major's facial expression never changed.

Bolt tossed a bill into the pot. "I'll bet a hundred."

"Any cards?" asked the Major.

Bolt removed the three low cards from his hand, placed them face down and pushed them to one side.

"Three."

Farrington raised his eyebrows as he peeled three more cards off the deck and dealt them to Bolt. Bolt picked them up, cupping his hands around them so no one could see them. His heart skipped a beat when he saw them. All hearts. The queen, jack and a nine. Damn, he had missed a royal flush by one lousy ace. But he still had a straight flush with king high. It was good enough to win if Farrington couldn't top him.

"I'll match you and raise you a hundred," said the Major calmly. He looked at Bolt, waited for Bolt's next bid.

Bolt noticed that Farrington hadn't taken any cards for himself. A bad sign. It could mean that Farrington was perfectly happy with the cards he'd drawn.

By the time they had raised the bet a couple of times, everyone in the saloon had gathered around the table to watch. Neither of the players looked at their cards again while the bidding continued.

The bidding went fast until they each had added five hundred to the kitty. With the chips that were in the pot, it was worth over two thousand dollars.

Bolt paused before bidding again. The Major was so sure of himself. It was possible he had a royal flush in another suit. Bolt had not seen him bid so quickly before.

Bolt raised another hundred, noticed that Farrington was also taking more time to think before bidding. Bolt couldn't figure the man out. One minute Bolt thought he himself had the winning hand, the next minute he wasn't so sure. Farrington kept him guessing. That's what made the Major a good player.

The bidding continued until Bolt had finally tossed his last hundred dollar bill into the pot.

"I'll see you," said Farrington evenly. It had been a gentleman's agreement that they would play only with the money they had showing. There was over three thousand dollars at stake.

The room became absolutely quiet as the crowd waited to see who would rake in the loot.

Slowly, Bolt spread his cards out in front of him.

The onlookers gasped at the show of hearts, started to whisper to each other, then became quiet again as they waited for the Major to turn over his cards.

Bolt's heart skipped a beat when he saw the confident smile that crossed Farrington's lips. Bolt took a deep breath, tried to control his nerves, but the man had him rattled. Bolt considered himself an expert at keeping a poker face, but he knew that his nervousness showed. And to make it worse the Major was toying with him and enjoying every minute of it.

Farrington leaned forward and looked at Bolt, his blue eyes twinkling with merriment.

"She's all yours," Farrington grinned. "You're a damned fine player. Best I've ever seen. It was a pleasure to play with you, Bolt. And worth every damned penny."

The crowd began to cheer, slap each other on the back. No one knew whether they were hooting for Bolt's victory or Farrington's sportsmanship, but it didn't matter. Everyone was in a joyous mood.

"Drinks on the house," called Amylou above the roar

of the crowd. She was pleased as punch at the outcome of the game. The word would spread about the good, clean game and the publicity could only help the business at her saloon. "Cole, come over and cash in these chips for Mister Bolt," she ordered her head dealer.

The customers in the saloon surged toward the long bar to collect their free drinks as Cole Megan made his way to the corner table. The dealer wore bands around just above his shirt sleeve cuffs to keep his sleeves out of the way when he was dealing poker. He sat down at the table, began sorting and counting the chips. Bolt noticed that the man had a fairly young face, but he was prematurely bald with just a ring of dark hair above his ears and around the back of his head. He had a dark thin moustache.

"Bolt, this is Cole Megan, my best dealer," said Amylou.

Bolt extended his hand, but Megan ignored him and continued to count. "Nice to meet you," Bolt said.

"Of course, when Major Farrington is playing, Cole doesn't have to deal," Amylou explained.

Bolt thought he detected a scowl on Megan's face. He evidently resented Farrington doing his own dealing. Megan's fingers flew as he whisked the poker chips toward the edge of the table as he counted. Bolt watched his fingers for a moment, fascinated by the blur of movement.

"There's twelve hundred and fifty dollars worth of chips here, Ma'am." Megan placed the chips in neat rows in the tin storage box, closed the lid. He opened the small cash box he had brought to the table, counted out the correct amount of money and handed it to Bolt. That left the cash box empty because it was used only for storing

12

the money when chips were purchased. Amylou insisted on keeping the chip money separate so that Megan could cash in the chips when the players were finished playing. Cole Megan was completely responsible for the money and the chips and he prided himself on the fact that he always came out right. His fingers were fast, but he was accurate.

Bolt stuffed the bills in his pocket along with the two thousand in cash that he had won. He had spent almost fifteen hundred in gambling stakes that night, so he had more than doubled his money. Cole Megan, still scowling, picked up the two tin boxes. Impulsively, Bolt dug in his pocket, fished out a twenty-dollar bill and stuffed it in the dealer's pocket.

"Thanks, Megan, you're a good man," he said. The dealer walked away with no more than a nod of his head.

"You didn't have to do that," Amylou said. "I pay him well."

"I thought maybe it would cheer him up. Is he always that sour?"

"Only when the Major's playing. I guess he's jealous, but don't worry about it."

"I hope Farrington will play me again. I feel a little guilty about taking so much money from him. He seems like a decent sort."

"Don't give it a second thought," she laughed. "He's got plenty more where that came from." Her laughter was musical, like tinkling piano keys. Her dark brown eyes glittered when she smiled at Bolt. She moved over closer to Bolt, put her hand on his. "You're really good, Bolt," she husked. "Where'd you learn to play like that?"

"Some things come more natural than others, I

13

reckon," he grinned. Her scent drifted over to him. He breathed in deeply, felt giddy from the jasmine aroma.

"What else comes natural to you?" she husked in a teasing manner. She scooted over closer to him, looked up at him with wide innocent brown eyes.

Bolt read the bold invitation in those eyes.

"I can think of a couple of things that come mighty easy to me," he grinned, teasing her back.

"Oh? Would you mind showing me?" She batted her eyes, mocking innocence as she moved even closer. She puckered up her mouth, then ran her wet tongue across her lips. Her hand slid across to Bolt's lap, found the bulge between his legs under the table.

Desire flooded Bolt's loins as he felt the warmth of her hand flood through his trousers to his manhood. He watched her tongue slide across her moist, glistening lips, felt his manhood begin to swell.

"Your room or mine?" he said in a low voice that cracked with desire.

"Yours would be just fine." She gave his manhood a gentle squeeze before she rose from her chair.

Chapter Two

"Come on back to my office," Amylou said. "I've got a couple of things to do before I can leave. Then I won't have to come back here tonight. Carl and Cole can close up tonight."

Bolt followed the dark-haired beauty to the back room. He liked the way her narrow green skirt clung to her body, accenting her high, flared buttocks. He liked the way her long, shiny hair bounced across her back as she walked. She left a fragrant, flowery scent in her wake and Bolt breathed in deeply as he walked.

Inside her office, she poured two glasses of brandy, handed one of them to Bolt. She removed a heavy cloth bag from her top desk drawer, excused herself long enough to collect the night's receipts from the till behind the bar. When she returned, she unlocked a small vault that sat in a corner of the room, partially concealed by a bookcase. She pulled several bulging heavy cloth bags from the safe, placed them on her desk, then locked the safe again.

"I don't want to leave all this money here," she explained as she stuffed the cloth bags inside a fancy hand embroidered valise.

A few minutes later, they stepped out into the cool night air, Bolt carrying the valise full of money in one hand, Amylou's arm looped through his free arm. They walked across the hard-packed dirt road to the Sundowners Hotel which was directly across from the Red River Saloon, right in the middle of the busy town of Houston.

"Feels like rain," Amylou said in a lilting voice, holding her hand out in the air to feel for moisture.

Bolt glanced up at the dark sky.

"No stars out tonight. We could get a little shower."

"We sure need it to settle the ground. Those afternoon dust storms we've had the past couple of days have made a mess of everything."

"I know. Since I've been in Houston, I've felt like I was chewing a mouthful of sand half the time." He withdrew his arm from hers, opened the door of the Sundowners.

Inside, the lobby was empty except for the desk clerk, Henry Jamison, who came on duty at midnight and worked through until eight in the morning, when his replacement came in. Jamison looked up when he heard the door open. He was a young man, way too heavy for his short frame. His clothes had to be specially made for him and even then, he always looked sloppy with his obscene belly hanging over his trousers. He wore red suspenders and they seemed to accentuate his fat bulge of blubber that circled his middle. His light brown hair was long and shaggy and with all the grease he used to keep it in place, it always looked dirty.

Bolt glanced up at the clock on the wall behind the clerk. It was later than he thought. Almost two o'clock in the morning.

"Good evening, Mr. Bolt," said Jamison, struggling to sit up taller so he could ogle the woman with Bolt.

Bolt noticed that Jamison's eyes traveled the length of

16

Amylou's body, his mouth hanging open like a drooling dog.

"Evenin', Henry. Any messages for me?"

"Nope. Your friend, Mister Penrod, came in a while ago. And he wasn't alone, if you know what I mean."

Bolt wanted to knock the shit-eating grin off the fat boy's face, but he ignored the crude remark.

"You have a nice one, Henry," Bolt said politely and ushered Amylou toward the stairway.

"You, too, Mr. Bolt. I *know* you will."

Bolt led Amylou upstairs to his room, quelling his urge to knock some manners into Jamison's head.

"I feel naughty coming to your room like this," Amylou said coyly after Bolt had closed and locked his door with the large metal key, and lit the lantern.

"You are naughty," he grinned, taking her in his arms and kissing her passionately.

"I mean the way that clerk looked at me like I was some . . . some hussy. And I nearly died when he said what he did."

"Don't pay no mind to that horny bastard. He's probably never had a piece of ass in his life."

"Ugggh! I wouldn't think so!" She wrinkled up her nose and made a face.

"He's probably peeked through plenty of keyholes, though, and jacked himself off." Bolt smiled.

Amylou shot a look at the keyhole and then began to laugh at the image Bolt's words conjured up.

"He probably can't even reach it," she giggled, "let alone see it."

Bolt loved her sense of humor, the way she was always gay and joyous. She had a zest for life that was rare in a

17

woman, especially in the west where times were hard. She was self-confident and Bolt liked that in a woman. He couldn't stand whimpering, whining women who wouldn't do anything for themselves. Amylou Lovett was the kind of woman he would choose for a wife if he were prone to settling down. But he wasn't. Not yet.

He set her valise down in the corner where his rifle was propped against the wall, right next to the chest of drawers. He opened the top drawer of the bureau, slipped his wallet from his pants pocket and automatically slid it under the neat stack of shorts and socks in the drawer. The wallet contained the two thousand in bills from the poker game. The rest of his money, the bills from cashing in the poker chips, was still loose in the same pocket because his wallet had been too stuffed to hold the other paper money. He was just about to empty that twelve hundred from his pocket and put it under the socks when Amylou came up behind him and wrapped her arms around his waist. She leaned her head against his shoulder, pressed her breasts against his back. Her hands traveled down his body, groped his manhood. She pulled him toward her so that her loins were jammed up against his buttocks.

He let her grope for a moment, then whirled around and held her in his arms. He kissed her, probed the wetness of her mouth with his hard, flicking tongue. She responded, slid her tongue along his, jarring Bolt with the electricity of her passion.

He scooped her up in his arms, carried her to the bed across the room, sniffing in her heady fragrance. She smelled like a rose garden on an early summer morning, like freshly cut hay in a dew-covered meadow. She felt good in his arms, light and supple, warm. Her smooth dress clung to her slender figure, showing off every curve to advantage.

He eased her down beside the bed until her feet touched the floor, but she kept her arms wrapped around his neck until he kissed her again.

"I want you so much, Bolt," she said, her velvet voice laced with lust. She began unbuttoning her dress slowly, watching Bolt's eyes as she did.

He unbuckled his gunbelt quickly, hung it over the bedpost near the pillows. When he came back to her, she had slipped the bodice of her dress down her shoulders, exposing full, firm, creamy breasts. Slipping a hand under one of the heavy breasts, he dipped his head, took a nipple into the moistness of his mouth. She gasped with pleasure that made her knees weak.

"Hurry, Bolt. I want you now!"

While she finished undressing, he jerked his boots off, tore at the buttons of his shirt, threw the shirt to the floor. He stripped out of his pants, let them fall to the floor. He stepped over to the lamp, blew the flame out.

They came together again, their naked bodies boring into each other with a searing heat.

"Do you want me, Bolt?" she asked softly.

"Very much," he husked. But he did not have to answer her. Blood surged through his manhood, causing it to swell and stiffen against her bare leg. She moved against it, caught it between her legs, urging it close to the lips of her sex-cleft. She wriggled her hips in a circular motion, then began an up and down motion when his swollen shaft pulsed against her sensitive lips.

He felt his throbbing manhood slide across the crease of her hot sex. His cock became even more rigid and the sticky fluid began to ooze from the slit on the flared head.

Gently, he pushed her over onto the bed, crawled in beside her. He leaned over to kiss her, felt the heat that radiated from her lovely body. As he slid his tongue inside her wet eager mouth, he reached down to her firm breast, took a nipple between his thumb and forefinger, squeezed it until she began writhing on the bed. He toyed with the rubbery tip until it hardened like a kernel of corn. He broke the kiss, dipped his head down to her breast, took the thick nipple into his mouth, laved his tongue across it until she trembled all over as if suddenly chilled by a cool breeze.

She groped in the darkness, found his rigid cock with her warm, delicate fingers. As she tightened her hand around the mass of swollen flesh, his cock twitched as if struck by a bolt of lightning. She stroked his cock up and down slowly, squeezing gently as she slid her hand up its length. The fires of desire raged in his loins. He sucked harder on her supple nipple, covered it with hot saliva.

She ducked away from his hot kiss at her breast, leaving his lips tingling with wet fire. Still clutching at the base of his cock, she moved around, dipped her head to his loins. With her other hand, she traced her finger across the tip end of his shaft, smeared the rich, slippery fluid across the mushroom head. Her breath was like a hot summer breeze on the tip end of his cock and because of the dampness of his juices, it both cooled him and warmed him at the same time. He shivered as if a feather had been drawn across his stomach.

She took his cock into her wet mouth, drew it deep inside. He felt a spear of passion slam into his loins. He ran his fingers through her silken hair, pulled her head tight to his loins. Her head bobbed up and down the rigid length of his manhood as she sucked it, letting her hot saliva cover the flesh. She sucked hard, until her cheeks caved in, until he thought he would explode inside her mouth. She took him still deeper, so deep he thought he could feel her throat.

When she finally backed away, he rolled her over on her back, positioned himself above her.

She spread her legs wide to receive him.

"Hurry, Bolt. I want you so bad I could scream."

He lowered himself to enter her. She arched her back like a wind-blown branch to meet him.

His swollen cock dipped down to the sensitive crease of her sex lips. She bucked as if shot with an arrow. He pushed past the lips, slid into the hot, steaming folds of her flesh. She thrashed and quivered as the first orgasm rippled through her loins like a flood tide.

"Aaaaahh," she panted. "Bolt . . . oh Bolt . . ."

He thrust into her steaming portal again with a gentle force. Her body undulated beneath him as she slammed her thighs up to meet his powerful thrusts. Her hips gyrated in a circular motion, then in a back and forth movement as she matched his strokes, wild in her passion.

He pumped his cock in and out of her steaming honey-pot, burrowing deeper into her flesh with every stroke. He jabbed at her with hard, fast thrusts, unable to slow down because of her continuing thrashing. She moaned, cried his name every few minutes as the orgasms overtook her again and again.

She did things with her loins that made him gasp for breath. It was as if she had spent her whole life preparing for this one glorious moment. She was like the most practiced harlot, expert at her craft. She was all women at all times. She was one special woman at this very erotic moment. Even from beneath him, she manipulated his body, his nerve-endings like a finely tuned guitar.

He knew he was about to spill his milky seed. He had to pause, slow down, or it would be over too soon.

"Don't stop," she cried, mindless in her passion.

He eased back into her burning flesh, plunged his cock in deep. He slid his hands under her buttocks, drew her loins up to him. He withdrew his swollen cock slowly, until the tip end of it was kissing her entrance, then plunged it all the way to the hilt. It went in deeper this time. Her muscles tightened around his cock like a vise, locking him deep inside her.

He plunged in and out of her wet fiery sex with renewed fury, increasing his rhythm, gripping her flared buttocks tightly.

"Yes . . . oh yes, Bolt. Do it to me."

"Do what?" he breathed. He wanted to hear her say the words.

"Fuck me, Bolt! Fuck me like you've never fucked anyone else."

His mind was lost in a sea of passion. He felt like he was floating somewhere above their bodies, watching every intimate detail of their love-making. Glimpses of her naked breast floated through his mind, the nipple hard and dark against the creamy white flesh of the breast. An image of her thighs darted across his mind, sweet delicate thighs that were spread apart to receive his probing shaft. He saw her furry mound that shadowed her most private, precious place of her being.

"More, Bolt. Give me more."

Her words brought him out of his fog.

He bored into her, smacked against her loins with fiery passion. He drove deep inside her as she tugged at him with gripping muscles.

She met his thrusts with her own upward thrusts, sucked him in deep, trying to keep him locked inside.

He rammed deep inside her, felt the heat that seared his cock. He stroked her deeper, faster, knowing he could not stop now until he reached that moment of sheer ecstasy.

The musk of their twin passions rose up to his nostrils. He breathed in deeply, was hypnotized by the mystical effect of its dank scent.

He jabbed at the tight sheath of her sex with quick, short strokes, panting loudly in equally short, rapid breaths.

Sensing what was about to happen, Amylou thrust her hips high up in the air, squeezed her buttocks together as hard as she could as she clamped her sex muscles tight around his driving shaft.

Bolt's body stiffened as he rammed his cock into her for the final thrusts as his seed boiled up and spilled over, splashing against the folds of her sex pot.

"Oh love . . . oh yes . . . yes . . ." he stammered as his cock pulsed and throbbed in the final burst of orgasm.

It was a long time before he could gather the strength to roll off of her sweat-soaked body. He winced as he withdrew the sensitive head of his already shrinking manhood.

They lay there side by side without speaking, basking in the afterglow of their love making, enveloped in a haze of contentment.

Finally he placed his hand on her bare thigh, gave it a gentle squeeze.

"You're some kind of woman," he sighed.

"You're not so bad yourself," she said in her musical

voice. She snuggled in closer to his naked body. "I was just thinking, Bolt. I don't know much about you. In fact, I only know two things about you."

"What's that?" He turned his head toward her, saw the dark outline of her face.

"You're a poker player and a lover. And an expert at both, I might add."

"Then you know everything about me," he teased.

"Did anyone ever tell you you're conceited, Bolt?" she giggled.

"I've been called worse."

Suddenly she sat upright in the bed.

"What was that noise, Bolt?"

"What noise?" He leaned over, reached for his pistol automatically. As his hand touched the holster in the dark, he paused to listen. And then he heard it.

"Rain," he said. "It's starting to rain."

"Oh, I love the rain," she sighed.

They lay back down and Bolt wrapped her in his arms, drew her body close to his.

Suddenly, nothing else mattered.

They fell asleep a little later to the sound of a gentle rain dripping on the roof, splashing against the window pane.

Chapter Three

The clanking metal sound was far away. Lost somewhere deep in Bolt's dream.

He stirred, rolled over in his sleep, his back to the door. His arm flopped across the bed, came to rest on smooth, bare flesh.

Startled only for a brief moment by the feel of warm naked skin under the weight of his arm and hand, he remembered the raw passion of the woman in his bed when they had made love a few hours before.

He listened for the rain, but it had stopped.

His eyes opened slowly, focused on the stark facial features of the lovely creature beside him. The first traces of morning light filtered through the curtain, fell across her bare curves, basked them in a gray pallor.

Beautiful, free-spirited Amylou Lovett. A woman who was sure of her femininity. A woman who knew when to be a lady and when it was better not to be.

He ran his fingers through her long silken hair that fanned out across the pillow. When his hand ran down across her bare shoulder, he wanted her again.

That's when he heard the metal scratching against metal sound again. He was awake this time and knew instantly what it was.

Someone at the door.

He stretched his arm up, reached for his pistol that hung holstered from the gunbelt slung over the bedpost.

He was too late.

"Stop right there, pilgrim!"

Bolt's head snapped around to look toward the door.

A tall man with a bandanna covering his face stood just inside the room, the pistol gripped in his hand aimed directly at Bolt's head.

The masked man stepped closer to the bed as two men behind him burst into the room, pistols cocked and trained on Bolt. They wore dark bandannas over their faces too.

"What the hell?" Bolt's eyes widened in surprise. The men had him outnumbered. He didn't dare move.

"Hope we didn't interrupt anything, sonny," said the man on the left. Bolt noticed that the man whistled when he talked like he had a hole in his throat. If he did, it was covered by the bandanna. He was also left-handed.

Amylou woke with a start, screamed when she saw the masked men with guns pointed at the bed. She reached down and clutched at the sheet, drew it up quickly to her neck to cover her nakedness.

"Just do what we tell ya and nobody gets hurt," said the tall man. He stared down at Bolt with dark beady eyes.

Bolt saw a trace of a scar on the man's left cheek. The scar was long enough to be visible above the black bandanna.

Bolt sat up slowly, inched over to the edge of the bed, keeping his hands shoulder high. Amylou threw a corner of the sheet over his lap. She turned her head slowly, glanced up at Bolt's pistol hanging above her head. She wondered if she could reach it if the three men were distracted.

"Don't even think about it, missy," the closest man warned.

26

She turned back and glared at him.

While the tall man was looking at Amylou, Bolt moved his foot slightly, spidered it along the floor until he felt his trousers. He eased them back ever so slowly with his toes, trying to scoot them under the bed, out of sight. He thought about the loose hundred dollar bills wadded up in his pocket.

"Watch it, Jake! There's his pants," called the man with the scratchy voice as he came around to the front. Bolt heard the wheeze in the man's throat when he breathed. Likely he had a bad lung rather than a hole in his throat.

"Shut up, you fool!" snapped the tall man whose name was Jake. He walked over next to the bed, stooped down to pick up the trousers. His feral eyes never left Bolt's. Nor did his pistol. "Yair," he drawled, "this is what we're lookin' fer." He tucked a corner of the pants under his right elbow, dug into a pocket, came up empty-handed except for a handkerchief. He quickly searched another pocket, drew out a couple of bills, then stuffed them back in the pocket. He tossed the pants back to the man on his left. "Here, take care of this."

The man behind him caught the trousers. When he holstered his pistol, Bolt noted that the man, who wore the leather wrist-bands, was packing a pair of six-guns, both with hand-carved grips.

"Search the room," Jake ordered the third man.

"That's all the money we have," said Amylou coldly. "Now get out of here and leave us alone."

"I don't believe you, missy."

"I think this is it," said the third man as he discovered Amylou's valise in the corner. He picked it up, carried it over to Jake.

"Open it up," Jake ordered. His eyes twinkled with a smug smile when he saw the contents. He glanced over at Amylou.

"Don't you dare take that money," Amylou said with fire in her eyes. "I'll see that you spend the rest of your born days in the pokey if you steal that, you lousy thief."

Jake and the other two men laughed uproariously.

"You really scare me, missy," said Jake.

Bolt started to lunge toward Jake to knock him off balance. But Jake shoved the pistol between his eyes at the first move.

"Kinda itchy, ain't ya, pilgrim?" Jake taunted.

"Go to hell, you bastard," mumbled Bolt.

"Oh, what language," Jake said, mocking astonishment, "and especially in front of this proper lady."

"Hey, some of the money's missing," shouted the man who had taken charge of Bolt's trousers. "There's no more than eleven or twelve hundred here."

"Where's the rest of it?" Jake asked as he glared at Bolt with dark slitted eyes.

"Me and my lady friend spent it," smiled Bolt. "Had ourselves a whale of a time."

"Don't pull no dumb-shit act on me," Jake threatened, his finger beginning to tighten around the trigger.

Bolt said nothing, but continued to stare at the tall man beside him. He knew they'd find his wallet, but he sure as hell wasn't going to tell them where it was.

Jake changed his tactics. He let the man with Bolt's trousers, Whit Stoneman, cover the pair on the bed with a pistol while he strolled over to the window, pushed the curtain aside.

The rising sun streamed through the window, lightening the room considerably. "Nice day fer a funeral," he noted.

Jake strolled over to the side of the bed where Amylou sat defiantly, still clutching the sheet to her throat. He shoved his pistol against Amylou's temple, looked over at Bolt.

"Now you gonna tell me where the rest of the money is?"

Bolt shot him a dirty look, rose from the bed.

"Easy does it, pilgrim," Jake said, "or she's a gonner."

Bolt moved slowly, started for the chest of drawers.

"No, Bolt," Amylou said, her voice strong with anger. "Don't give it to him. Let the bastard shoot me. That'll bring half of the town in here."

Bolt admired her spunk, but he couldn't risk having her shot because of his money. He'd come across men like this before. They didn't give a damn whether they shot a person or not just as long as they got what they wanted. Another man's life meant nothing to them. They had no conscience, only greed. And in the end, they always got what they deserved. That was a lesson he had learned from his preacher father many years ago.

He opened the dresser drawer, dug under the stack of socks and brought out his thick wallet. He handed it to Jake, keeping his hand just far enough away so that the tall man would have to reach for it. He figured he could grab Jake's hand when he reached for it, get him off balance.

Jake didn't fall for it. "Give it to him," he said, nodding toward Whit Stoneman.

Stoneman stepped forward, snatched the wallet from Bolt's hand. His cold eyes were such a pale blue, they looked gray as he stared at Bolt. Bolt wondered what the rest of his face looked like. Shaggy blonde hair jutted out from under the man's battered hat.

Stoneman pulled the thick stack of bills from Bolt's wallet, thumbed it as he made a quick count.

"It's all here, unless he's got more money stashed someplace else."

"Do you?" Jake asked.

"You've already stripped me bare," Bolt said. "What do you want? Blood?" He hoped they wouldn't decide to search his room more carefully. Yes, he had more money stashed. His "trail money," as he called it. About three thousand dollars worth. He had it hidden in various places, scattered throughout his belongings. Some five hundred stuck in his possibles bag, a thousand dollars in each of his saddlebags, tucked into false linings and another five hundred in his bedroll.

"We got what we came for," said Jake. "Let's get the hell out of here. It's already light outside."

Stoneman stuffed the money from Bolt's trousers and wallet into Amylou's valise, dropped the wallet on the floor and secured the latch on the valise. He carried it by a small leather handle as the three men started to back out of the room, their pistols still aimed at their victims.

"Hold up a minute," Jake called to the others. "I want to make sure these two lovers don't go anywheres for a while."

"You want me to tie 'em up?" asked the man with the wheeze.

"No, I've got a better idea. Bolt, is that your name?"

"You heard it right."

"Walk over to the window and open it."

Bolt hesitated until Jake pointed the pistol at Amylou again. He stared at the tall man, wondered how he got the scar on his face. He did as he was told, opening the window about four inches.

"All the way smart-ass," Jake said, bored with Bolt's lack of cooperation.

Bolt pushed the window up as far as it would go. He saw the wooden balcony outside the window, realized what Jake was getting at.

"Now climb outside," Jake ordered. He moved the gun closer to Amylou's head.

Bolt hunched down, crawled through the window, stepped out onto the narrow rickety balcony.

"Now you, missy. Outa that bed. Join your lover out there."

Amylou glared at Jake, got out of bed, still clutching the sheet around her naked body. She moved toward the window, the sheet trailing behind her.

"Just you, missy. Not your fancy nightgown." Jake whipped the sheet away from her in one jerk.

She tried to cover her bare bottom as Bolt helped her out onto the balcony. Jake followed her to the window, holstered his pistol once she was outside and quickly slammed the window shut, locked it from the inside.

Bolt watched the three men inside his room. They gathered near the window, laughed at the pair out on the balcony, stark naked. Then the man with the two six-guns began talking to Jake. Bolt heard the murmur of their distorted voices, but couldn't make out the words. He cursed the fact that the men were wearing bandannas over their faces, their mouths, because he was pretty good at reading lips. If he could only make out what they were saying, it might give him a clue to their identity. All he knew was that the tall man was called Jake.

He turned his back to the window, pretending not to pay any attention to the robbers, but he kept his head turned slightly so that one ear was tuned toward the window. He leaned his head back a little until it was just inches away from the windowpane. Concentrating with all of his effort, he was able to make out a few words. "Good work." ". . . got it . . ." "bash 'em," or "Bascomb." He couldn't be sure. The men got a little louder as they ignored the two naked people on the balcony.

"Let's go." It was Jake's deep voice.

"Won't Bascomb be pleased as shit!" said the wheezer.

So it was Bascomb, Bolt thought, obviously a man's name. He turned around in time to see the three masked men leave the room, close the door behind them.

When she heard the door slam shut, Amylou quickly turned toward the window, trying to hide her naked body.

"Can we get back in?" she asked.

Bolt struggled with the window, couldn't get it to budge.

"They locked the damned window, but we'll get in."

"Maybe we could break it."

"Yeah, if we had anything to break it with."

Amylou turned around, looking for something hard that they could knock the window out with. She heard laughter from below, looked down over the railing. She was horrified to see the passersby on the street below stop and look up. She quickly covered her breasts with her hands, doubled over to hide her private parts from the gawkers. The gathering crowd laughed when she did this. She blushed, wished there were not so many people on the street at this early hour.

"Hurry, Bolt, we're drawing a crowd."

"There's not a damned thing up here to break the window with unless I can pry part of the railing loose."

32

He tugged on one of the boards, but it didn't give. It was hardwood, stronger than it looked. His efforts brought a cheer from the crowd, but he couldn't work any of the boards free.

"Come on," he said, "I know how we can get back inside."

He walked along the narrow balcony to the next room. He knew it was Tom Penrod's.

Still doubled over, Amylou followed him, walking on tiptoes on the damp wood. She threw one arm across her large breasts, attempted to cover her flared buttocks with her other hand.

The men below whistled, hooted and hollered for her to show it all. A couple of matronly women turned their heads, tried to drag their husbands away. It was becoming a circus and Amylou didn't like being the main attraction.

"Oh, Bolt," she whispered, "this is so embarrassing."

"Hell, you've got a beautiful body. Don't worry about it. Besides, we'll be inside quicker'n you can shake your sweet ass at those horny bastards down there. This is my friend's room, thank God." He turned around and looked at her, almost broke out laughing himself at her awkwardly twisted body. "Hey, you got goose bumps on top of goose bumps. You cold or just scared?"

"Nervous. It is a little chilly out here but I hadn't noticed it until you mentioned it."

Tom's window was closed, but the curtain was open. Bolt pressed his forehead against the window, tried to see inside. He saw the bed where Tom and his blonde woman friend were still sleeping. They had a blanket over them so they looked like two lumps.

Bolt rapped on the window with his knuckles. He saw

33

Tom awaken with a jerk of the head as he glanced at the door. Bolt knocked again, harder. Tom looked in his direction, jumped out of bed, startled until he saw who was at his window. His lady companion, Tess Hummer, woke with all the commotion, screamed when she saw the naked man at the window.

Tom doubled over in laughter. He was wearing shorts and an undershirt. He glanced back at Bolt, saw the naked girl cringing beside Bolt. He pointed at the couple, slapped his leg and laughed even harder. His friend was always getting himself into a jam, but this was the funniest thing he'd ever seen.

"Let us in!" Bolt shouted.

Tom turned his head slightly, cupped a hand behind his ear, pretending not to hear Bolt's plea. He shrugged his shoulders, indicating he didn't understand a word Bolt had said.

"Open up, you lousy bastard!"

"Oh," Tom mouthed silently. He stretched his arms out, fingers curled up, made the motion of raising the window.

"Yes, yes," Bolt called in a louder voice. "Open the window."

Tom put his hands on his hips, grinned as he shook his head, then went back to the bed and crawled in beside the puzzled Tess.

Chapter Four

Frustrated by his friend's playful antics and total disrespect for the seriousness of the situation, Bolt pounded the closed window, called Tom Penrod every name in the book. And a few he had just invented.

The crowd that had gathered on the street below cheered at the drama that was being played by the naked couple on the balcony.

Bolt pressed his head against the windowpane again, exposing his bare ass to the gawkers below. He saw Tom grin and wave from the bed.

"Damn you, Tom! Let us in!"

Tom got out of bed, walked over to the window and stood right in front of Bolt, with only the glass barrier between them.

Bolt heaved a sigh of relief, thought his friend was going to open the window at last. Instead, Tom stood there in baggy shorts and flexed his muscles, began doing exercises, raising outstretched arms above his head, clapping his hands together once, then lowering his arms to his sides again.

When Tom added leg exercises to the routine, jumping up and down, Bolt glared at him, made the sign of wringing Tom's neck. Tom continued the jumping jacks and Bolt made another gesture, one of kicking his friend in the groin.

Tess Hummer sat on the edge of the bed. Dressed in a

provocative blue nightgown, she was now laughing at the crazy antics of the two men. Amylou was at the window, shaking her fist at Tom.

Tom finally relented and opened his window after unfastening the latch. He helped Amylou through the opening. She was still trying to cover up her bare breasts, the furry mound of her sex. Once inside the room, she dashed across to the bed, sat down on the end of it and snatched the blanket, wrapped it around her.

"You son of a bitch," Bolt said as he climbed through the window to the final cheers of the crowd.

"With that act, you should join the medicine show," Tom laughed. He slipped into a pair of trousers, threw a shirt on and buttoned it.

"We've been robbed, Tom," said Bolt, turning away from the two women on the bed. "A lot of money. Run downstairs and see if you can see the crooks. They were wearing black bandannas. Three of 'em. They might still be in town. I'm sure they figured it would take us a long time to get back inside." He gave Tom a dirty look when he said it.

Tom slipped into his boots, not bothering with socks. He opened the door and ran down the hall.

Bolt dashed to the open door, yelled at his friend. "Hey Tom, send the clerk up here with a spare key to my room, will ya?"

A refined looking couple, just coming out of their room across the hall, stared at Bolt's naked body in the doorway. The elderly woman gasped in horror, slapped her hand to her head to shield her eyes from the obscene sight. "Well, I never!" she snorted.

"I don't know what this world's coming to," said the gray-haired man, leading his wife down the hall. "These

36

youngsters and their orgies!"

Bolt slammed the door shut, rummaged through Tom's bureau drawers until he found a pair of trousers. He stepped into them, buttoned the fly. The pants were about three inches too short, but Bolt didn't care. He grabbed a shirt from Tom's closet, put it on.

"I've got some of my clothes here," said Tess, who had been staying with Tom for the past three days. "I'm sure I can find something to fit you."

"Anything," said a grateful Amylou.

"What happened?" asked Tess, selecting a simple housedress from the closet, a long narrow full skirt to go under it.

Amylou stood up, took the slip from Tess, whom she knew. She slid the silky slip over her head, pulled it down over her naked body. A little small for her, it clung to her voluptuous breasts, her flared hips. She stepped into the dress that had buttons from the high neckline to a few inches below the waistline. The skirt was full enough to flow over her hips easily, but the buttons at the bustline threatened to pop from the strain of the full breast.

"Three masked thieves broke into our room and robbed us at gunpoint," Amylou explained.

"How terrible! I would have been frightened out of my wits. Did they get much money?"

"My cash receipts for the past month and all of Bolt's poker winnings."

"Does the name Bascomb mean anything to you, Amylou?" Bolt interrupted.

"It damn sure does. It means trouble. Why?"

"Those crooks mentioned the name, more than once. Who is he?"

"Ordway Bascomb, the biggest trouble maker I've

37

ever met."

"You know him?" Bolt's eyebrows shot up.

"Not really. He came into the Red River Saloon some four or five years ago, when my father was still living and operating the saloon. I was only fifteen or sixteen at the time, but I'll never forget him. Bascomb got into a poker game and nearly tore the place apart when he lost. It took all of my father's savings to put the saloon back together again. Whew, does that man have a temper! He's been run out of more Texas towns than a cattle rustler at roundup time. After he broke up the saloon, I heard that he was run out of Austin, then San Antonio."

"Where does he live now?"

"I don't know. He heads a renegade bunch that specializes in robbing people crossing the Colorado River. Those three who stole our money must be part of his gang. The Texas Rangers have hunted high and low for that bunch, but they are elusive. Funny thing is, Ord Bascomb used to be a Texas Ranger himself. Guess that's where he learned all the tricks. Anyway, he turned as bad as an apple at the bottom of the bucket. And nobody can find him. He just seems to appear out of thin air, make his strike, then disappear again. He and his bunch have robbed stage coaches, payroll wagons and single riders. But Bascomb always seems to know which stages are carrying large sums of money, and he seems to leave the poor people alone and strike only when wealthy riders are crossing the Colorado. I've heard more terror talks about that man from visitors who pass through town. He seems to have eyes everywhere."

"Does he ever kill his victims?"

"Yes. I've heard gory accounts from survivors. As long as the victims cooperated with Bascomb, he seemed content to take their money and let them go unharmed. But if anybody gave him any lip, he didn't hesitate to shoot them dead on the spot. Or torture the poor people to death. That's more his style. I've heard that he turns livid with rage if anybody back talks him and the more a victim balks, the worse the torture. I wish the Rangers could find him and lock him up forever."

"Sounds like a charming chap."

"I'm surprised at his boldness in coming into a big town like Houston, though. He usually operates out in desolate country. Why would he or members of his bunch come here?" Suddenly, Amylou became sick to her stomach when she thought about it and realized the answer to her own question. "Bolt! He knew about my cash receipts! Bascomb knew about your poker winnings!"

"How would he know unless he was there?"

"As I said, he's got eyes everywhere! It must have been one of my employees! Yes, I've been betrayed by one of my very own employees."

"Now, wait a minute, Amylou. Let's think this thing through. There were a lot of people watching that poker game. Any one of them could have been in cahoots with Bascomb."

"But what about my money?" she argued. "Only the people who work for me know that I was saving my cash receipts to make my mortgage payment. No one else would know that I had that much cash with me."

"Would any of them steal you blind?" he said, trying to calm her down.

"None of them, that I know of. They all do their work with little complaining and I pay them well."

"What about the glitter gals who work for you? Any of

them got a beef with you?"

"No. They're treated decent. Besides, none of them know my financial situation at the saloon. I've got to get that money back. The money in that valise represents survival for me. I have my payroll to meet and a heavy mortgage on the saloon due at the end of the week. Unless I get my money back, I will lose everything I own."

"I'll guarantee we'll get the money back. Now, just exactly which one of your employees know your financial situation?"

"Well, my head bartender, of course. Carl tallies up the receipts every night before he leaves. So does, Cole, the dealer you met. Both of them know I have a mortgage payment due."

"Anybody else? The other bartender, another dealer?"

"No, they don't know much about the business. The other bartender leaves his cash receipts in the till, lets Carl total it up at night. There's Loretta Sweeney, my singer. She helps me with the books, but she's above suspicion. She's my closest friend."

"Nobody's above suspicion, Amylou, when it comes to this much money. Greed does funny things to a person."

Tom came back into the hotel room at that moment.

"I didn't see 'em," he said. "No trace of 'em and nobody seems to know who they were. The only information that I could get was that three masked men rode through town about a half hour ago. They were heading west and they were joined by six other riders at the edge of town. They all rode out like they were in some kind of hurry."

"Nine men, huh?" Bolt said, thinking what his odds were. "Tends to complicate matters a bit. Did you get an extra key to my room?"

Tom dug a skeleton key from his pocket, threw it at Bolt.

"Thanks, Tom. I'll return your clothes as soon as I get my gear together."

"You're not gonna track nine men by yourself, are you, Bolt?" Tom asked, knowing the answer already. "Don't you think this is a matter for the law to handle?"

"Ha!" chirped Amylou. "The local sheriff would look the other way if he knew it was my money that was stolen."

"You sayin' he's crooked, Amylou?" Bolt asked.

"No. It's just that I'm beneath the law's contempt. Occasionally, I need a little law and order over at the saloon, but Sheriff Connors won't give me a hand. He won't even send over one of his deputies. It seems he doesn't like a woman running a gambling house, especially one who keeps glitter gals on the payroll. I've tried to explain that I inherited the business from my father when he died, but Sheriff Connors has a deaf ear."

"Then I go after Bascomb and his bunch by myself."

"Do you need some help?" Tom asked.

"I don't know yet. I'll let you know. If he's as good with the disappearing act as Amylou says, I have a feeling it'll take some time to find him. I'd better take some provisions and I'll have to pick up my horse at the stable, get him saddled up. It'll take a little while to get ready. Stick around."

Bolt and Amylou walked next door to Bolt's room. Bolt unlocked the door with the skeleton key, checked the door thoroughly, examining the keyhole, the latch around it before he closed the door.

"Those three men didn't break in here like I thought," Bolt said, shaking his head.

41

"What are you saying?" Amylou asked.

"They unlocked the door just like anybody else."

"But how . . ."

"With a key. Look, there's no sign of a scratch or a tear at the keyhole. The handle wasn't forced and obviously they didn't break the door down. No, they had the key to my room and I intend on finding out how they got it."

"That creepy desk clerk?"

"That's my guess." Bolt quickly took off Tom's short trousers, put on some of his own, after stepping into a pair of clean shorts. He grabbed a clean shirt from his closet, slipped into it, then put fresh socks and boots on.

"Bolt, I want to go with you. To catch the thieves, I mean."

"No, Amylou. It's a job for a man."

She whirled around, fire in her dark eyes.

"I'm sick and tired of hearing people say that. I can ride and shoot as good as any man. And if the sheriff won't help you, and I know he won't, then you're going to need an extra hand. You can't face all those men by yourself."

Bolt almost laughed at her logic. Two against nine was not much better odds than one against nine.

"No. Tom said he'd ride with me. I'd feel better if you'd stay here and wait for me."

"Well, I wouldn't," she stormed. "After all, part of that money belongs to me! I insist on going with you and that's final!"

"You win," Bolt grinned, tossing his hands in the air in a signal of surrender.

"Just give me time to go home and change into riding clothes and get my pistol and horse."

"It'll probably take me a litle longer to get ready, so

meet me at your saloon in about a half an hour. While we're there we can check to see if any of your employees are missing. If one of them set up the robbery, then it's likely he, or she, left town with Bascomb. Right now, I'm going to talk to the desk clerk. Come on, I'll walk downstairs with you."

The clerk, Henry Jamison, looked up with sleepy eyes when Bolt stopped in front of his counter. According to the clock on the wall behind him, he still had fifteen minutes to work.

"You folks have a good night?" He winked and there was something obscenely lewd about the expression on his fat puffy face. He looked at the front of Amylou's dress, saw the buttons that were about to pop.

Amylou walked right on by the desk, disgusted by the crudeness of the corpulent man. "I'll see you later, Bolt."

"Yair." He turned to the clerk. "You see three men come in here about an hour ago?"

"I don't know what you're talking about." Jamison rubbed his eyes, stretched his blimp-like arms, then sat up taller, his body rolling in blubber.

"I think you do," Bolt challenged. He waited for Jamison to respond but the clerk only shook his head, his thick jowls swinging back and forth between his double chin. "Three men entered my room about an hour ago and robbed me and Miss Lovett of all of our cash."

"I didn't see nothin', no sir, not me." He held his thick hands up in the air, continued to shake his head. He looked even more unkempt than he had when Bolt had talked to him in the middle of the night.

"I didn't say the men *broke* into my room, Jamison. I said they *entered* it. They used a key to open the door. And

43

I think you gave them that key." Bolt hunched his frame over the counter, leaned closer to the fat man, an accusing look in his eyes.

"They musta used a skeleton key, then. I sure as heck didn't give them three men a key."

"Then you saw them?"

"Hell, no, I didn't see 'em. I been asleep most of the night. Ain't much to do at night, you know."

Bolt didn't believe him.

"I'll take your word for it, Jamison, but if I find out you're lying, you're gonna lose some of that baby fat in a hurry."

"Oh, no, Mr. Bolt, I ain't lyin'. I'm plumb sorry about your money. How much did they get away with?"

"Enough," Bolt said coldly, backing away from the counter.

"You gonna chase 'em down?"

"I plan to."

"Well, don't you worry none about that pretty Miss Lovett while you're gone. Leave her here at the hotel, in your room, if you want to. I'll see to it that she's safe from any further attacks or robbers."

Henry Jamison had a hungry, animal look in his eyes. Bolt knew what the fat man was thinking. He recognized lust when he saw it.

"Thanks anyway, Jamison. But I think she'd be safer with me."

Chapter Five

"You sure you don't want me to go with you?" Tom asked.

"Yes," said Tess Hummer who had changed out of her blue slinky nightgown into a plain daytime frock. "I'll go with you, too, since Amylou is going."

"Thanks for the offer," Bolt said, "but I think that would slow us down too much. It might get a little hairy out there and I don't want to risk any lives."

"But, you're risking Amylou's life," Tess sulked.

"I told Amylou it would be better for her to stay here and run her business, but she's pretty independent. To the point of being bullheaded, actually. She says it's her money and she's determined to help get the money back. Not much I can do about it. She said if I didn't take her, she'd just follow me."

"Anything I can do to help while you're gone?" Tom asked, a troubled look on his face. He knew what Bolt was facing and even though Bolt was just about the fastest shot he knew, the odds were too dangerous, even for Bolt's gun. Nine against one, or two, if Amylou could shoot.

"Hell, I wish you'd have been that cooperative about opening that damned window, you prick," Bolt laughed, trying to ease Tom's fears. His own as well. "But I could damn sure use your help right now. I have to carry all my gear over to the stable, get Nick saddled and ready to ride.

I could use a strong body."

"I knew you'd find some task that would use up all my intelligence. Bolt, wouldn't it be easier to bring Nick over to the hotel, load your gear from here?"

"Easier, maybe, but I'm in a hurry. Those bastards already have an hour on me. I don't want to mention any names, but if a certain friend hadn't taken so long to open his window . . ."

"I know, I know. Let's get going. Tess, you wait right here for me."

"I'm not planning on going anywhere," she cooed, batting her eyelashes at Tom seductively. "I'll wait in bed if you want me to."

"God, woman, we got to stop to eat once in a while," Tom grinned. "Can't you wait till after breakfast?"

"That long?" she purred as Tom and Bolt left the room.

Bolt and Tom went next door. Bolt had his gear all laid out on the floor next to the door.

"You're not taking your bedroll?" Tom asked.

"Not planning to be gone that long," Bolt smiled smugly.

Bolt leaned down, picked up a dark sock that was on the top of the gear, handed it to Tom.

"What the hell you givin' me a smelly sock for?"

"Handle it with care," Bolt said. "That sock contains all my cash, except for a few bucks in my pocket."

"Then they didn't get all your money?"

"No, just what I won in the poker game. But fifteen hundred of the winnings was mine in the first place."

"How much is in here?" Tom hefted the sock in his hand, regarded it with more respect.

"Three thousand. I don't want to leave it in my room

46

while I'm gone and I sure as hell don't want to take it with me and give those bastards a chance to get this, too."

Tom looked at his friend for a moment.

"It's gonna be bad, isn't it?"

"Won't know until I find them, but I reckon I been in worse jams."

Tom paused, thought about the times Bolt had helped out some poor woman in distress, the trouble he had gotten in because of it.

"Is it worth it, Bolt? Is any amount of money worth the risk?"

"No. It's not the money, Tom, you know that. It's the principle of the thing. These men are bad, like a rotten potato in the bottom of a burlap bag. The rot spreads, affects those around it. Same with this Bascomb guy. His greed spreads to others, to his bunch. If he isn't removed, the whole sack of potatoes rots and stinks. You heard Amylou. Bascomb terrorizes innocent victims, tortures them if they try to stand up for their rights. It's wrong. Men like that shouldn't be allowed to live. Until this kind of thing is stopped, no one will feel safe to live in the west. He's got to be taken out and if the law can't, or won't, do it, then I will."

He handed Tom the possibles bag and his rifle to carry. Then he lifted up the heavy saddlebags, slung them over one shoulder. The filled canteen went over the other shoulder. Even though he hoped to be back before sundown, his saddlebags were loaded with provisions: beef jerky, hard tack, dried beans, a tin of coffee and the utensils he might need if he had to trail the men any length of time. He also carried a small blanket and a clean shirt inside the bags.

Outside, Bolt noticed that the ground was still muddy

47

from the rain during the night. He stepped out to the street, examined the thick mud in front of the hotel, around the hitching post. He didn't find what he was looking for.

He detoured around the side of the building, staring at the ground. He went on around to the back of the building.

"Bolt, have you totally lost your mind? The stable's in the other direction."

"There they are! The tracks!"

Tom moved in closer and looked down.

Bolt walked around the area near a fence behind the hotel.

"Yep, this is where those bastards stashed their horses while they were robbing us. You know that ground was hard packed before the rain. These are fresh tracks."

Bolt followed them for a ways, along the back of the mercantile store next door to the hotel. Then the tracks went along the far side of that building, back on to the main street, where they headed west through town. Bolt could tell the thieves had picked up speed when they hit the street because the hoof prints were deeper. He turned and smiled at Tom.

"I think my job's going to be a lot easier than I thought. Thanks to the rain."

They turned east and walked a block to the stable. The sky was still overcast and Bolt was grateful. The cloud cover would help preserve the tracks a little longer and he didn't fancy riding out under a blistering sun.

At the livery stable, Bolt didn't see the boy who took care of the horses. He set his saddlebags and other gear down near Nick's stall, then stepped in to pat his horse on the rump. "Good boy. We're going for a fast ride, just as soon as I can get you saddled." Nick raised his head, snorted at the sound of Bolt's voice. Bolt ran his hand across Nick's flanks before he turned away.

"Ronnie!" Bolt called as he glanced around the stable, into the other stalls. "Anybody here?" He walked to the gate at the back of the large room that smelled of hay and manure, spotted the stableboy out back. Ronnie Hall, who couldn't have been more than fourteen years old, was dipping a bucket into a large watering trough. Five empty buckets were at his feet.

"Hello, Ronnie," Bolt called.

The boy looked up and grinned when he recognized Bolt. His face was covered by freckles and a piece of straw jutted out from his mop of red hair. He set the bucket down, started toward Bolt.

"I didn't hear you come up," he said, his green eyes twinkling.

Bolt liked the boy and paid him extra to take special care with Nick.

"I just came to get Nick. Wanted to let you know. I have to ride out of town, so I'm not sure when I'll be back. Might even be tomorrow."

"Want me to saddle him up fer ya?"

"No, I can do it. Tom's here to help me. You're busy. Just didn't want you to think someone stole my horse."

"Oh, hi, Mister Penrod. You need your horse too?"

"No. I'm staying here."

"O.K., Mister Bolt. Have a good trip." Ronnie turned back to the water trough.

"I'll try to," Bolt said softly, more to himself than to the stableboy.

Bolt found Nick's saddle and saddleblanket. Tom threw the blanket across the horse's back, smoothed it out, held it in place while Bolt slung the saddle up in place.

Leaning over, Bolt started to fasten the cinches. He took the time to see that they were not too loose, not too tight.

When he stood back up, he saw the shadow at the front entrance of the stable. He squinted his eyes, tried to make out the big man's features, but he couldn't tell who it was. The light was behind the man, throwing his face in shadow. Bolt's hand automatically went to his holster, hovered above the butt of his pistol.

The man stepped inside the room and Bolt saw the silver badge attached to the man's shirt.

"Good morning, boys," said Sheriff Connors.

Bolt eyed the man, didn't like what he saw. Connors was tall with a large barrel chest that strained against the fabric of his shirt. The sheriff swaggered as he walked toward the two men, kept his two thumbs tucked into his waistline where his shooting hand was within easy reach of his pistol. It was a threatening gesture, a pompous show of authority that Bolt found loathsome. He'd known a hundred lawmen just like him, who were more impressed by their tin badge, than they were interested in upholding justice. He could see why Amylou didn't like the man.

"Morning," Bolt mumbled politely as he lowered his hand, came around from behind his horse, straightening the horse blanket and literally ignoring the swaggering sheriff.

"Good morning," Tom said cheerfully, not liking the sheriff any more than his friend did. "Nice day if it don't rain."

The huge man seemed even more massive as he

stepped up to Bolt, blocking Bolt from picking up his saddlebags.

"You planning to take yourself an early-mornin' ride?" the sheriff drawled smuggly.

"Yep. That's what I'm planning to do." Bolt kept his voice even, noncommital. The fumes of whiskey radiated from the thick lips of the sheriff when he spoke, nearly knocking Bolt backwards. He started around the big man to get to his saddlebags.

Again the sheriff blocked him.

"You boys wouldn't be wanted by the law, would you?" The tone of his voice was condescending.

"I don't think that's any of your business," Bolt said, irritated at the sheriff's crudeness.

"I think it is. You know who I am, don't you?" He pointed to his badge, tapped it with his forefinger.

"Yeah," said Bolt. "I think the name's Connors, if I'm not mistaken."

"So, you do know who I am. Well, I run a clean town here in Houston and I aim to keep it that way. We don't allow no riffraff here. I've been watchin' you two since you rode in here a few days ago and if my suspicions are right, there's a wanted out on you. I'm going to have to ask you to stick around until I can check it out."

"I'm just going for an early morning ride, as you said. I'll be back by the time you do your checking if you need me, which you won't."

"No, you're not leaving town. Now, boys, I'm trying to be as polite as I can, but you've got to understand my position."

"Why, that's quite all right," Bolt said, mocking the sheriff's patronizing attitude. "I'll just ride my horse around the town. He needs the exercise." He started for the saddlebags again, knowing his time was precious.

"You wouldn't be needin' those bags just to ride around town, now, would you? No, you're not taking that horse anyplace. If he needs exercise, let the stableboy do it. You go anywhere and you go on foot." He backed away, smugly satisfied that his orders would be followed.

"You're not stopping me, Sheriff. I'm taking my horse. You haven't got anything on me or my friend. You can't hold us."

"You boys don't seem to realize the importance of this badge." He jabbed at the shiny star again. Then his hand shot to his holster, whipped a Colt .45 out.

Bolt hadn't expected it. The sheriff's hand had been a blur and Bolt hadn't reacted fast enough to draw his own weapon.

"Well, since you put it that way . . ." Bolt stepped closer to Connors. He saw the smug look on the man's face. He knew he had him. With a quick, smooth motion, Bolt jerked the pistol from the surprised sheriff's hand. As he took the pistol, he turned sideways, rammed his shoulder into the big man's chest.

Sheriff Connors staggered backwards, tripped and fell to the ground. His elbow landed in the middle of a horse turd on a small pile of hay that had dropped from the stableboy's shovel when he cleaned the stalls.

"Next time, Connors, I'll kill you."

The sheriff looked up at him, dumbfounded. He tried to regain his composure by brushing the dust from his shirt. He glanced down at his arm. His nostrils flared as he smelled the stench on his shirt sleeve. Anger flushed in his face. Slowly, he pulled himself to a sitting position, gave Bolt a dirty look. Then he looked down, shook his head as if in defeat.

Bolt watched him, saw it coming.

With a sudden movement, the sheriff leaped up from the dirt, tried to ram Bolt's body with his head.

Bolt's arm shot up in the air, then came down with force as he cracked Connors over the temple with his own pistol butt.

Connors gasped, collapsed to the floor, unconscious.

Tom stepped in to see if the sheriff was really out cold.

"I hope you know what you're doing, Bolt."

"I do too." Bolt set the sheriff's pistol down next to his head, after removing the bullets. "Hey, Tom, can you finish up here and bring Nick over to the Red River Saloon. I want to go on over there right away."

"What's your hurry?"

"Amylou's meeting me there."

"Won't she wait?"

"Of course she'll wait, but there's something phony about Connors coming in here checking on us. How'd he know we'd be at the stable getting a horse? If my hunch is right, we're dealing with more than Bascomb and his men. I think the sheriff is in on this, too."

"Think so?" Tom glanced down at the barrel-chested man sprawled in the dirt. "What does that have to do with Amylou?"

"She thinks one of her employees set her up. If the sheriff is in on this and one of Amylou's employees, then that means that not all the men rode out of town. Obviously Connors knew we'd be here. Who knows what's happening over at the Red River. Amylou might be in danger."

Tom looked down at the unconscious sheriff again, checking his size. He looked back up at Bolt.

"Shit, Bolt, what if Connors wakes up before I'm

through. I'd hate to tangle with that ornery ox."

"Just work a little faster than you did opening that window and you'll be all right," Bolt grinned.

"Will I never hear the end of that? It was just one of those priceless moments in a man's life when he can witness another making a real ass of himself."

"Go to hell," Bolt joked. "Don't worry. I gave Connors a pretty good whack. He'll be out for a while and his pistol's empty. Just keep your eye on him. There are only a couple of things to load. The saddlebags, my rifle, the canteen. And check with Ronnie to see if Nick's had any water this morning. If not, just give him a little bit."

"Yair, go ahead. I'll bring Nick over."

"Thanks, and, Tom, when you get there, tie Nick to the hitchrail out front. But stay with him until I come outside. I don't want anyone tampering with my gear while I'm inside the Red River."

Bolt left the stable, dashed up the street.

He didn't like the way things were going.

His odds were diminishing all the time.

And he hadn't even left Houston yet.

Chapter Six

Bolt checked his pocket watch just before he entered the Red River Saloon. It was already after nine o'clock in the morning. The robbers had such a head start on him now that it was no longer a matter of chasing after them. It was now a case of tracking them down. If they were half as slippery as Amylou had indicated, it might take a while. And even if he found Bascomb and his bunch, there was no guarantee they would still have the money with them. By now they would have had plenty of time to stash the loot, or even split it up and go their separate ways for a while, at least until the next robbery.

That was the way with such thieves. Rob a stage or a bank, hold up a train, then split the money, live high on the hog until they got the opportunity to rob again.

He didn't have much to go on at this point. Three robbers who had worn masks to cover their identities, the name of one of them, Jake, and one more name: Bascomb. And the fact that six riders had joined the trio of thieves at the edge of town and headed west. Besides that little bit of information, all he had were his hunches and suspicions. If any of Amylou's employees had disappeared then he'd have another piece to the puzzle.

The Red River Saloon was almost deserted that time of morning. Bolt was relieved to see Amylou was sitting at the table in the far corner, the same table where he'd played poker the night before. Dressed in riding breeches and a matching jacket, a bright yellow blouse, she was chatting with two elderly gentlemen who were playing dominoes and drinking coffee. She smiled and waved when she saw Bolt come in, got up from the table and headed in his direction.

There was no hustle and bustle of activity in the saloon like there had been the night before. No glitter gals, no music, no musty smell of warm beer.

Bolt glanced around the large room, saw that there were only two other customers besides the domino players, two men who looked like they were nursing a hangover with whiskey and beer chasers. Charlie, the daytime bartender stood behind the bar, polishing glasses with a clean towel. A young, lanky boy swept the floor at the opposite end of the room. Missing were the people Bolt wanted to talk to: Carl Anders, Cole Megan and the singer Amylou had mentioned.

"I'm all ready to go," Amylou said. "Charlie brought my horse around front and I had Mrs. Harrington at the cafe next door pack us a box lunch."

"What about Cole and Anders?" Bolt asked in a low voice. "Either one of them leave town?"

"I just saw Cole eating breakfast next door and I'm sure Carl is in his room. He lives here at the saloon, in a room in the back. I like to have somebody staying here all night when we're closed."

"I'd like to talk to them before we go."

"Yes, me too, but I was waiting for you." She turned to the boy who was sweeping. "Charlie, would you go back and tell Carl I'd like to talk to him. Then go next door and tell Cole the same thing. Tell them it's important."

Charlie leaned his broom against the wall, walked to the back.

"What about your singer? Have you seen her?"

"Loretta? Sure, she's in my office, working on the books. In fact, she's figuring up my payroll right now."

"Let's go talk to her."

"Let me tell you what I know about her. She's been working for me for about a year. She came to Houston from Fort Worth. She's a fair singer, but the customers love her. And she's a terrific bookkeeper. She also happens to be my very best friend."

Bolt stroked his chin, looked down at the floor as he thought about what she was saying. He had seen Loretta singing when he first came into the Red River last night, but he hadn't paid any attention to her.

"Was Bascomb ever in Fort Worth?"

"You mean when Loretta was there? I couldn't say. He's been tossed out of most of the towns in Texas, so he's probably been in Fort Worth."

"What did she do before she came here?"

"Now, that, I don't know, but I think she's got a shady past. She won't talk about it at all except to say that her husband ran off with a whore a couple of years ago. I really think she was a prostitute in Fort Worth, she applied for a job as a singer. She said she could help me with my bookwork if I didn't need a singer. In fact, she said she'd do anything to make a living *except* being a prostitute."

When Amylou opened the door to her office, a pretty red-haired woman glanced up from the desk.

"Loretta, this is a friend of mine, Jared Bolt. Bolt this is Loretta Sweeney."

"Oh, the big poker winner," Loretta smiled, extending her hand. Her smile didn't ring true to Bolt. It looked pasted on.

"News travels fast. Pleased to meet you."

"Bolt wants to ask you a couple of questions," Amylou said.

Loretta looked up at Bolt, waited for him to speak. Bolt noticed, when he got a closer look at her, that there were hard lines on her face and that she was much older than he first thought. She wore too much makeup, probably to cover the lines, make herself appear younger. Bolt guessed her to be about forty, give or take a few years.

"Do you know a man named Bascomb?"

"Can't say that I do."

Her answer was too quick, Bolt thought. She didn't even take time to think about it.

"Where'd you go after you finished singing last night? Who'd you see?"

Loretta's head snapped back as if she'd been struck. Her eyes widened for a brief moment, then squinted to angry slits.

"What is this?" she snapped. She turned and looked at her boss. "Amylou, how dare you bring this man in here to ask me such personal questions!"

"He didn't mean it to sound personal, but he has to ask the questions," Amylou tried to explain.

Loretta glared at Bolt with cold blue eyes.

"Mister Bolt's wanted by the law. Did you know that?" she spat.

It was Bolt's turn to be surprised. He wondered how Loretta knew that. It had been so long ago, he had almost forgotten about it himself.

"No, I didn't," Amylou said softly, looking at Bolt, waiting for him to say it wasn't true.

"Well, you should pick your friends more carefully." Loretta flipped her long red hair back away from her face,

58

stuck her nose in the air.

Amylou was embarrassed, didn't know what to say. Finally she spoke to her close friend. "Loretta, Bolt and I were robbed this morning. The thieves got all our money, mine and Bolt's. And you, more than anyone else, know how desperately I need that money. We think we were set up—by someone who knew how much money we had."

"And you're accusing me?" she said haughtily.

"Nobody's accusing you of anything, Loretta," Amylou said, trying to soothe her friend's ruffled feathers.

"He probably set up the robbery himself," Loretta said in a mocking tone. "Just so he could get your money. He and that skinny friend of his probably arranged it."

Cole Megan entered the office just then, followed by an angry Carl Anders.

"What's this about a robbery?" Megan asked, picking food from his teeth with the fingernail of his forefinger.

"Shit, you woke me up," grumbled Anders, running his fingers through his tousled blonde hair.

Bolt moved back to make room for the two men, leaned against the wall while they got settled. Anders, the bartender, plunked his lean body down in a straight back chair next to the desk, hunkered down until he was reasonably comfortable. Megan leaned against a file cabinet across the small room from Bolt.

"Let's begin at the beginning," Bolt said, then went on to explain about the early-morning robbery and his and Amylou's subsequent suspicions. He watched the three employees carefully as he talked.

Loretta Sweeney remained cool and distant as if she didn't give a damn about it, as if the robbery was something that didn't concern her. She tapped her pencil on the sheaf of papers on the desk, showing her irritation and impatience at being interrupted.

The dealer, Cole Megan seemed calm and interested, although when he realized he was under suspicion, he did a fast draw with his pistol, twirled it around in his fingers and jammed it back in the holster. He did this several times as if he was practicing his speed. Megan looked Bolt in the eye the whole time and Bolt took his movements as more of a threat than a practice session. The man was fast, no doubt about it.

But Carl Anders was the one with the quick temper.

When Bolt concluded his explanation by saying that no one was above suspicion in the robbery until it was solved, Anders jumped up from his chair, his face crimson with anger as he stood in front of his boss.

"Amylou, I quit! You can take this job and spit on it! You can draw my pay on the spot! I don't need this kind of shit from a no-account!"

"Whoa. Now slow down, Carl," Amylou said. "Bolt didn't say you did it. You have a job here as long as you're loyal and in the clear."

"No, I won't be treated this way after all the years I've worked for you!"

"Carl, you're going to explode one of these days if you don't learn to control your temper," Amylou said, patting the bartender on the shoulder. "Look, we're all upset, but right now we're just trying to figure things out. If you're innocent, you've got nothing to worry about."

Anders returned to his chair, but he was sullen about being a suspect.

Cole Megan took a step forward, twisting his thin moustache, his eyes glaring at Bolt. His hand fell slowly from his face to his side, hovered above his holster.

"If you're accusing me of robbing Miss Lovett,"

Megan said, his eyes level on Bolt's, "then you'd better draw on me now. That's too serious a charge to lay down for, stranger."

"I'm not accusing anyone," Bolt said, "but someone set up the robbery and I mean to find out who."

Cole looked at Loretta, who was watching the interplay with more interest now. Then he looked back at Bolt.

"Who are you to mix in here, with a price on your head? Looks to me like you got a fox to guard the henhouse, Miss Lovett."

That was twice somebody had mentioned that Bolt was a wanted man. Bolt didn't like it. Someone had been mighty busy checking on him.

Amylou glanced down at the floor, then lifted her eyes to look at Bolt. She was beginning to have her doubts about him.

Bolt didn't answer her unasked question. Instead, he turned and walked out of the room. Megan was spoiling for a fight and he wasn't going to give him the satisfaction. As far as he was concerned, any one of the three employees could have been in on the robbery. Each of them had certain traits that made them look guilty as hell.

"I'll be with you in a minute, Bolt," Amylou called, determined to go with him after Bascomb.

"I'll be outside," he answered.

"You through with us, Amylou?" Carl asked.

"Yes. Sorry we woke you up, but it was important."

He mumbled something and shuffled off. Megan followed him out the door.

"You really going with him?" Loretta asked.

"I have to. If I don't get that money back, I'll lose everything."

61

Loretta leaned over, opened the bottom drawer of the desk and pulled out a small hideaway derringer, handed it to Amylou.

"Here, take this. In case Bolt turns out to be the doublecrosser."

"But I don't need that. I've already got a pistol." She opened her jacket to show Loretta the pistol that she wore in the gunbelt holster.

"You may not have a chance to draw that pistol when you need it. Bolt looks like he has a way with the women and I think you've already fallen for his charms. Men like that can be mean and dangerous. I know. Better to have a little gun that he doesn't know about. Keep it where you can get to it in a hurry."

Amylou shuddered. Grateful for her friend's help, she took the small pistol, concealed it in her waistband.

"Thanks, Loretta." She hugged her friend, then went to join Bolt.

Tom was waiting for Bolt when he walked outside. Nick was loaded and ready to go. The sun had come out and Bolt could already feel the heat building.

"Tom, I want you to stay behind, keep an eye on the saloon and the people who work there. Especially Loretta Sweeney and the night bartender and dealer. If they do anything funny, follow them."

"Loretta, the singer? Hmmmm, this could be more interesting than I thought."

"Don't tell me you've got the hots for her. She's old enough to be your mother, almost."

"Hell, I'll take 'em any age. I ain't particular."

"No, you're certainly not. Besides, I don't think she likes you."

"Why not?"

62

"She called you my skinny friend," Bolt laughed.

"Nothin' bad about bein' nice and slim. If she doesn't like me now, she will by the time you get back."

"I said to keep your eye on her, not screw her."

Amylou came out of the saloon just then so the boys stopped their good-natured banter.

"Amylou, do you have an extra room where Tom could stay while we're gone?"

"You think we'll be gone that long? I thought we'd return before it gets dark."

Bolt noticed that Amylou was nervous and fidgety, which was not like her at all. Usually she was independent, full of life, to the point of being spunky.

"We may be, but I'd feel better just knowing Tom was here."

"Yes, of course," she said softly. "He can use the spare room upstairs. Tess can show you where it is, Tom. She stayed there for a while after her folks died."

"Thanks. You ready to ride, then?" He looked over at her, thought she looked pale. "You don't have to go, you know."

She took a deep breath, climbed up on her horse and smiled at Bolt.

"I'm ready."

Ord Bascomb reined back on his horse, held one hand in the air, signaling the other riders to stop.

His right-hand man, Randy Billings, rode up alongside him.

"You gonna cross the river?" Randy asked.

"No, I think we should split up. I don't think we have to worry about a posse chasin' us unless Miss Lovett was able to round one up, but you can bet your last sawbuck that Bolt feller will be on our tail."

Amylou's fancy valise hung from a leather thong tied to Bascomb's saddlehorn. It was dusty and stained from the mud that had splattered on it earlier that morning.

"I wouldn't worry about him, Ord. He's only one man."

"Yes, one man. With a reputation. I've heard a lot of tall tales about that young man. Most of 'em true, I reckon. He's fast and he's tricky."

"How do you want to split up? Each of us go our own way for a few days?"

"I'm going to head south for Eagle Lake. I'll take you and Leacock and Gough with me. Send the rest of them up north."

"Good idea. Keep the men in two groups. Let Bolt take his choice which one to follow." Randy slapped his leg, laughed, exposing crooked, stained teeth. His face was ugly, deformed by an eyelid that stayed half-open, half-closed all the time and a long, crooked nose that had been broken too many times.

Bascomb waved his arm, signaling the other riders to join him.

"Water your horses, boys. Fill your canteens. We're going to split up now."

The outlaw bunch filled their canteens in the Colorado River. It was muddy after the rain, so they had to go upstream a ways before they found clear water. When they finished watering their horses, they gathered around Bascomb for their orders.

"Ernie and Dan, you ride with Randy and me to Eagle Lake. The rest of you head north for a couple hundred feet, far enough for your tracks to show you're going in the opposite direction from us. Then double back like you're going to Houston, far enough to give Bolt a merry chase. Then head straight north to Etinger. I'm planning on Bolt following you five. Kill Bolt on sight. Leacock, when the job is done, report to me at Eagle Lake."

"What if he brings a posse with him?" asked Ben Cripps, a short, thick-muscled man.

"Then kill them too."

"What if he follows you instead of us?" asked Nestor Turner, who was not too bright, but mean as hell.

"Then you won't have to worry about it. I'll take him out myself. Might be kind of fun to meet the bastard face-to-face. I haven't tortured anyone for a long time."

Bascomb was tall and muscular with thick shoulders and large strong arms. A lock of his dark shaggy hair fell across his wide forehead. He was constantly brushing it back out of his eyes.

Whit Stoneman, one of the trio who had robbed Bolt and Amylou stared at the muddy valise that hung from Bascomb's saddlehorn.

"What about the money?" Stoneman asked. "You gonna split it up now?"

Bascomb, who had mounted his horse again, leaned over, untied the thong that held the valise. He brought the bag up, steadied it on the saddle in front of him. He opened it, took out the cloth sacks of money, hefted them in the air. Then he snatched the loose money, held it up.

The hardcases cheered when they saw the green backs and the sacks that held Amylou's money. They waited, wide-eyed, anxious for Bascomb to count the money and dish up their share. They knew Bascomb would take one-fourth of it off the top for his cut in masterminding the robbery, but still, they would get a good chunk of money for a few hours' work.

"No, Whit," Bascomb said smugly. "Then I couldn't

65

be sure you'd stick around long enough to take care of Bolt. We'll just wait until that's done, then we'll split it up when you all get to Eagle Lake." He jammed the loose money into the already stuffed cloth sacks, tied the strings tight, then jammed the sacks into his jacket pockets.

"It ain't fair," said Hoke Talley, one of the other robbers. "Three of us risked our lives to get that money."

"You want it now, you come take it," Bascomb threatened.

Talley thought about it for a minute, but changed his mind. He knew what Bascomb did to anyone who crossed him. He got on his horse and headed north. The other four riders followed him.

Bascomb flung the empty valise into the river. It splashed, then started bobbing along with the current. He turned his horse south, jabbed his spurs into its flanks.

Randy Billings looked down at the hoof prints in the drying earth. He laughed harshly.

"Bolt's going to shit his britches when he sees all these tracks," he cackled.

"Yes," said Bascomb solemnly, "and it will be the last time he does."

Chapter Seven

At the edge of town, Bolt picked up the trail of the three robbers. He saw where the other riders had joined them, where they had all ridden west on the well-used muddy trail.

The mud was almost dry now, but the tracks were fresh enough to be clear and distinct. Bolt climbed down from Nick, tossed the reins up to Amylou to hold while he examined the tracks more closely. There were so many of them that they all tended to merge together. He walked further up the trail, trying to isolate some of the hoof prints. A hundred yards up the road, he was able to pick out some individual tracks as the riders had spread out.

Amylou followed quietly behind him, leading Bolt's horse.

He finally found what he was looking for: some tracks that were different enough from the others that Bolt would know he was following the right ones when he got out on the open trail. One set of tracks was larger than the others, indicating that the horse was bigger and required a larger set of horseshoes.

He spotted another set of tracks that was different. One of the horses was dragging a hind leg. That would mean the horse was either lame and favoring that leg, or deformed.

"Is Bascomb a big man?" Bolt asked, thinking about the big tracks.

"I don't remember," Amylou said. "I only saw him once and everybody looked big when I was that age. All I remember is his cruel face, his mean eyes."

Bolt looked up at Amylou as she talked. He thought she looked more like a young boy than a full-figured woman in her riding breeches and floppy man's hat that held her long dark hair tucked underneath it. But she was beautiful, no matter what she wore.

When he took the reins from Amylou, he noticed that she did not make eye contact. Something was bothering her. Or maybe she just wasn't as brave as she pretended.

They rode at a good pace, not too fast to tire the horses, but fast enough to make good time. Bolt slowed every once in a while to make sure he was still following the right tracks.

The sun burned into them as they rode along the barren trail. The mud had dried quickly, but the hoof prints were like permanent indentations in the earth. Amylou remained quiet and subdued as they crossed the open prairie.

It was almost two in the afternoon when Bolt saw the Colorado River up ahead. Scattered clumps of cottonwoods jutted up from the river's edge. They were a welcome sight after all the scrub pine and brush they'd ridden through. The trees were tall enough to provide some shade while they watered their horses. It was the hottest time of the day and the heat was almost unbearable because of the lingering mugginess following the downpour during the night.

"Oh, that shade feels good," Amylou said as they rode up to the edge of the river, stopped under a small grouping of trees.

"Bascomb's bunch stopped here, too. Look at all those tracks."

"Do you think they crossed the river?"

"Hard to tell till I do some checking. Are you hungry?"

"Yes, but do we have time to stop?"

"The horses need a rest. No telling how long we'll be riding." He took his hat off, rubbed the sweat from his brow with his sleeve. "We should eat something. We didn't have breakfast, you know." Bolt dismounted, brushed the trail dust from his trousers.

"I'll get the box lunches out of my saddlebag. Mrs. Harrington made some roast beef sandwiches, two apiece. And there are some boiled eggs, fresh fruit and a sack of her special ginger cookies." She threw her leg across her horse and slid down to the ground.

"A sandwich will be plenty. We don't want to ride on a full stomach. There's a blanket in this saddle bag. You can spread it out in the shade. And could you fill our canteens? I'm going to check these tracks out, see if I can figure out which way those bastards went from here."

Bolt walked away from the spot where all the hoof prints blurred together, where Bascomb and his men had stopped to discuss their plans and exchange bitter words about the stolen money. He had already noted the tracks that went down to the bank of the river, but he wouldn't know if the outlaws had actually crossed it until he sorted out the tracks that fanned out from the place where all the horses had milled about earlier. Most likely the men had just led their horses to the river to drink, like he would have to do with his and Amylou's horses.

Walking south, he was finally able to pick out separate

sets of tracks at a point where the men had ridden side-by-side for a short distance, as if they had been carrying on a conversation with each other. There were four sets of tracks. Four horses. Four riders. The lame horse was in this group. He wondered where the other riders had gone. Retracing his step, he walked back to the place where all the tracks merged together. Then he followed more tracks that went in the opposite direction. He walked north, parallel to the river for a long way, until he was well out of sight of Amylou. These tracks were harder to separate because the outlaws had apparently ridden single file. He finally picked out the oversized hoof prints, the horseshoes that were bigger than the others. The tracks turned east, heading back toward Houston. It was at this point that he was able to make out five separate sets of prints.

He wouldn't go any farther by foot. He knew what he wanted to know, for now. The gang had split up, and he had to decide which group to follow.

The decision would be a hard one. He wanted to get the three bastards who had robbed him, but he also wanted to find Bascomb. Knowing how outlaw gangs worked, Bolt figured Bascomb had all the money with him. But his reason for getting at Bascomb went deeper than the money. He wanted to stop Bascomb from robbing any more riders or stagecoaches crossing the Colorado. He wanted to stop the corrupt man from killing and torturing innocent victims.

He wanted to rid the west of heartless, degenerate men like Bascomb so people could breathe a little easier, so they could live without fear. His convictions were so intense, he was ready to take on the whole west by himself.

Amylou got the thin blanket from Bolt's saddlebag, spread it out in the shade of the cottonwoods. Then she took the paper bag containing their lunch from her own saddlebag, placed it in the middle of the blanket.

As she moved about, she kept her eyes fastened on Bolt as he walked south, looking down at the ground. She was suddenly frightened to be alone with the man she loved. What if Loretta was right about Bolt? What if he had set up the robbery himself just to get her money?

No, she told herself, that couldn't be true. Bolt hadn't known that she was going to take her cash receipts to his room the night before. That had been her idea. But maybe he had figured that she had a lot of cash on hand and he had used his charm to gain her confidence. Maybe he and his friend, Tom Penrod had a scheme going whereby they bilked innocent women out of their savings. After all, they did appear to be drifters. She'd only known Bolt for three or four days and he'd swept her off her feet. If this was true, if Bolt was a swindler, then he could have paid the three masked men a few dollars to break into his room and take the money. Maybe that explained how the bandits knew how much money to look for. And Tom certainly hadn't been too concerned about the two of them being locked out on the balcony, stark naked. In fact Tom had laughed about it. Maybe that was part of the plan, too, to humiliate her.

Another thing, the robbers hadn't broken into the room, Bolt had said. They had used a key. Maybe Bolt had arranged for them to have a key or maybe he hadn't even locked the door in the first place.

She watched Bolt carefully, smoothing the blanket out more than was necessary, as he leaned down to examine the ground more closely. If this was all a hoax to get her money, then he wouldn't need her anymore. Maybe he planned to kill her. Maybe he was looking for a place to bury her. She patted her tummy, felt the small pistol that was stuck in her waistband, but it was little comfort to her just then.

She watched him, not wanting to believe that he was a thief, a swindler. The thing that bothered her the most was that both Loretta and Cole Megan had said that Bolt was an outlaw, a wanted man. She wondered what he was wanted for, if their accusations were true.

Bolt turned around just then, looked in her direction, then started walking back toward her. His eyes were cold and hard, piercing as he stared at her.

Amylou's heart pounded in her chest. Her hands began to tremble. She closed her eyes tight, afraid for her life. She opened them again, watched Bolt walk toward her. Her hand was at her waistband, but she didn't think she could shoot him if she had to.

Bolt walked right on by her, headed north, stopped when he had gone a hundred yards or so. He turned right, going slow to examine the prints. Finally, he disappeared from sight. Suddenly she was afraid that he would leave her alone out there. But that was crazy thinking. She was so confused at that point, she didn't know what to think anymore.

She took the canteens from the saddlehorns, decided to fill them while Bolt was out of sight.

As she approached the edge of the river, she saw a flash of color, like a piece of cloth, near the bank of the river. As she got closer, she realized it was her valise. She dashed down to the river, her heart thumping, her hopes high. The bandits had dropped her valise. Maybe the money was still inside.

72

"Bolt! Bolt!" she called, forgetting all about her fears. "I've found my valise!"

Bolt ran up a minue later, just as she stooped down to retrieve the dirty, wet satchel. He saw the look of joyous anticipation on her face as she lifted it from the ground.

Water dripped from the soggy satchel as she drew it to her body. She tore at the top of it, found that it was already open. She jammed her hand inside, felt the mushy, waterlogged fabric. Her hand searched desperately across the bottom of the bag, into the corners.

Bolt saw her expression change from anticipation to profound disappointment.

"Damn it! It's empty! The money's gone." She was on the verge of tears as she threw the valise to the ground, kicked it into the flowing river.

"Don't be too disappointed, Amylou. You didn't expect them to leave the money here, did you?" He put his arm around her shoulder, drew her close as he started walking back toward the blanket.

A lot you care, she thought, her anger flaring. She jerked away from him, moved her hand to her waistband.

"I thought maybe they had dropped it," she said managing to keep her voice under control as she stepped away from him.

Surprised by her coldness, Bolt walked on ahead of her. He spotted the canteens on the ground where she had dropped them when she saw the valise. He knew she hadn't filled them when he picked them up. He carried them back to the river, filled them while he thought about the change in Amylou. The water was fairly clear and cool.

When he was finished, he hung the canteen straps over the saddlehorns, plunked himself down on the

73

blanket. Amylou dug two sandwiches out of the sack, handed one of them to Bolt without looking directly at him. Then she scooted back, to the other side of the blanket.

"Come sit by me," he said, patting the blanket next to him. He saw her body stiffen as she unwrapped the white butcher paper around her sandwich.

"No, I'll sit across from you so I can watch you."

"Watch me what?" he laughed. "Eat? What's wrong with you, Amylou. I'm your friend."

"Are you?"

Bolt didn't like the tone of her voice.

"O.K. Spit it out. What's eating at you?" He took a bite of the tender beef sandwich, looked her in the eye.

She lowered her head to avoid his gaze, thought for a moment, then looked at him with soft, searching eyes.

"Is it true what they said about you? Loretta and Cole? Are you really a wanted man? Are you an outlaw, Bolt?" Her last question was almost whispered, as if she was afraid that saying it out loud would make it true.

"Some call me that."

She winced but said nothing.

He explained how he had killed two brothers, both lawmen, both crooked as they came. And both times had been in self defense. The first lawman he had killed, Reed Wilkins, had brutally beaten his wife Belinda. Reed was trying to kill both Belinda and Bolt when Bolt fired the fatal bullet. Then Reed's brother Maynard, who was a mean, dishonest marshal, had tracked him down. Bolt had blown him away to save his own ass. The brothers' father was Judge Wilkins from Coffeyville, Kansas and the judge had posted bounty money for Bolt's capture, printed up wanted posters, declared Bolt an outlaw.

"That doesn't seem fair," Amylou said, listening intently.

"It wasn't, but nobody promised me this life would be easy. Tom Penrod and I are also wanted for robbing a bank about that same time. Only that was a trumped up charge. We only took money that a pipsqueak banker in Fort Scott owed us. We sold Norvell a herd of cattle and he tried to cheat us out of our money. So we just went to the bank and politely took it—at gunpoint." Bolt smiled when he reflected on that situation. Norvell had been scared shitless, but Bolt and Tom had extracted exactly what was due them.

"How long ago was that?" Amylou said.

"Several years ago. Long enough for me to have forgotten about it."

"You mean that's all you're wanted for and there's still a price on your head?"

"I reckon there are still a few old wanted posters floating around. Hell, they printed enough of them."

"Well, I think it's terrible that you were ever considered an outlaw." She took delicate bites from her sandwich while she listened to his story.

"You know, Amylou, anybody can pin a label on you. It doesn't much matter whether they're right or wrong. Other folks tend to believe that label, and that's a fact you have to live with. Yes, I killed two lawmen, two brothers who would have killed me first if they could have. Their father, Judge Wilkins, tagged me as a murderer, but if his sons had killed me instead, the judge would have said that they were just doing their duty. Funny thing. Lawmen and outlaws are cut out of the same mold. They're just on different sides of the fence. Labels are like name-calling. If you're living right, the names don't bother you."

"I guess I misjudged you, Bolt," she said, smiling warmly. "When I heard Loretta and Cole say that you were wanted by the law, I guess I began to have my doubts about you. In fact if I hadn't wanted to get my money back so damned bad, I wouldn't have come with you."

"Money isn't everything, Amylou."

"Maybe not to you, but I worked hard for that money and I have to have it to pay my bills."

Bolt finished his sandwich.

"I'm not so much interested in getting the money back as I am getting the men responsible for the robbery. I have a special contempt for men who use other people for their own gain. Like Bascomb. He may think he's a big, powerful man, but he couldn't exist if he didn't steal from innocent people and if he didn't have men to do his dirty work. To be a man, you can't use someone else. That's what Bascomb's doing."

"You mean like me making money from the prostitutes who work for me? I guess that's using someone else for my own gain, although I make very little money from them. Most of it comes from the saloon."

"No. It's not the same thing," Bolt assured her. "I run a couple of whorehouses myself . . ."

"You do?" She was constantly amazed by Bolt.

"Yes, but I don't think of myself as using the girls. I run it as a business, but I don't force the girls to work for me or become prostitutes. They choose their own life. I just make it easier for them. They're free to do whatever they want. That's what I'm talking about. If everybody could be free to do their own thing without stepping on other people's toes, it would be a lot better world to live in."

"That'll never happen, will it?"

"No. There'll always be men like Bascomb around to spoil things." He stood up, walked toward his horse. "We'd better get going."

"Which way are we going?"

"I think we'll follow the riders who rode north, although they cut back east. There are five of them and I figure Bascomb wants all the protection he can get. Besides, I picture him as a big man and one of the horses is wearing bigger shoes than the others."

"That doesn't mean anything, does it?"

"Probably not." He grinned at Amylou, drew her up in his arms. "If either one of us had any money, we could flip a coin to see which way to go."

"Oh, Bolt, I want you. Now!"

"You owe me one then," Bolt smiled. "And when this is all over, I aim to take you up on your offer."

He hoped he would still be alive to collect.

Chapter Eight

Thick, dark clouds hung above them, threatened to dump a late afternoon shower on them. Lightning streaked the bleak sky off to the east. Ten seconds later they heard the distant rumble of thunder. They were both grateful for relief from the hot blistering sun.

The trail Bolt had chosen led them on a wild goose chase for nearly an hour as the tracks went north, then east toward Houston, then north again, and finally swung in a wide circle before they headed due north.

"The bandits are either drunk or lost," Amylou had said earlier.

"Probably a little of both," Bolt had laughed.

It had taken another hour of hard riding before they spotted the first signs of civilization.

"That a town up there?" Bolt asked as he slowed his horse.

"Looks like it," Amylou said, straining her eyes to scan the horizon. She saw the buildings off in the distance.

"Got any idea what it is?"

"Yes. That's a small trail town called Etinger. I might have known they'd ride out here."

"Why?"

"Etinger is a pretty rough town. Full of hardcases and men on the dodge. It's pretty dangerous to go in there. I hear there's no law at all in Etinger. That's why it's so popular with the outlaws."

"You want to wait here for me?" Bolt asked.

She looked around at the flat desolate country around her.

"No. I've come this far. I'm not about to give up now."

They rode toward the town slow and easy, watching their backtrail, checking to both sides and ahead of them for any sign of sudden movement.

Bolt's stomach knotted up in a hard ball when they got close enough to see the horses and riders moving along the main street of the town. He wondered if any of them were the men he was looking for.

A broken-down stagecoach perched on broken wheels at the edge of town like a symbol of the decadence of the small community that harbored fugitives. Its wooden frame was splintered, weathered from days of sitting in the sun and rain, its frame rusted.

Bolt glanced at the decaying hulk of the stage as they approached it, then looked away from it to study the men who walked and rode on the road that ran through the town. He wondered if any of them were waiting for his arrival. They would know he was coming. Otherwise they wouldn't have gone to so much trouble to try and disguise their trail. None of the men he could see were looking in his direction. He glanced up at the rooftops, didn't see anyone up there.

His attention was focused so far ahead of him, he nearly missed the movement just ahead of him, to his left.

When Bolt was just ten feet away, Ben Cripps stepped out from behind the dead stagecoach, opened fire with a rifle.

Startled, Bolt clawed for his pistol. It came out of the

holster already cocked by the time it was waist high. Bolt squeezed the trigger with lightning speed.

"Ride, Amylou! Fast!" Bolt yelled as he turned his own horse around.

His bullet just barely missed the short, muscular man and he stepped back behind the stage.

Ben Cripps had shot too fast, without taking aim.

Suddenly there were two men firing at him with rifles. Nestor Turner had joined Cripps, as they both dashed out in front of Bolt's horse. Two bullets fried the air, whizzed by Bolt's head.

He made a quick decision. He glanced around, saw that Amylou was already riding away from the town. Bolt jerked Nick's neck around, spurred him in the flanks, rode straight toward the two gunmen.

He fired once, which caused the two men to duck to miss his bullet. He saw the short man's hat fly up in the air as the bullet caught it, whirled it around.

Cripps and Turner were not able to get another shot off because they had ducked away from the fire. They recovered, aimed at Bolt. Before they could fire, they saw Bolt and his horse heading straight for them. A second later, Bolt drove his horse between them, forcing them to jump back, out of his way so they wouldn't get run down.

Bolt's plan worked, at least for the brief time it took him to ride between them and head toward the town. He chose that path because he knew Amylou was going the other way and he didn't want any stray bullets to hit her.

For a few seconds, neither man could shoot as Bolt passed between them. They held their Winchesters poised, ready to shoot while they struggled to keep their balance.

A minute later the air burst with gunfire again. The

Winchesters boomed, one after the other. The men were aiming high because Bolt was up on his horse. Too high to hit him.

He heard two bullets whiz over his head. He jerked Nick's reins to the left, urged him over to the edge of the street, where he rode just a few feet away from an empty building at the edge of town. He knew he would be a harder target for the shooters.

Another shot rang out from behind him. An instant later he heard the bullet thunk into the wood of the building, slightly behind him. If the shot had been six inches to the right, it would have smashed into the back of his head, ripping his skull apart.

The next bullet came closer. It ripped through the loose fabric of Bolt's left sleeve, just barely grazing the skin. He felt a slight burning sensation a couple of inches below his shoulder.

He saw a side road up ahead. If he could reach that in time, he could duck in there, use the building for protection.

The bullets came at him, one after the other until it was suddenly quiet.

Bolt whirled around in the saddle to see what was happening.

Both gunmen were out of ammunition, were trying to reload with fumbling bullets.

Bolt made his move. He reined Nick around, did a 180 degree turn and rode toward the men, his finger curled around the trigger, ready to shoot when he could get a good shot.

Nestor looked up, saw Bolt coming at him. He dropped his Winchester, made a dash for his horse which was stashed behind the rotting stage. He snatched his pistol out of his holster as soon as he was atop the horse.

It took Ben Cripps a few seconds longer to realize that Bolt was gunning for him. He ran for his horse, tried to mount it while he still held the Winchester in his hand. Awkward in his attempt to juggle the rifle and still climb up in the saddle, he finally let go of the bulky weapon, let it fall to the ground, pulled himself up in the saddle. He slammed sharp spurs into his horse's flanks, took off in a hurry, following Nestor Turner on the path that led out of town.

Bolt saw Amylou up ahead of the two gunmen. She had stopped, turned her horse around to see if Bolt had been hurt. He couldn't shoot just yet because he might hit her by mistake.

He chased them down, riding on past Amylou who had her hands at her mouth, her eyes wide with horror.

He took careful aim, shot at the closest man. His bullet caught Cripps in the back. Cripps flew out of the saddle, fell off his horse. His foot caught in the stirrup. The horse dragged him a few feet before he was able to free his foot. His body slammed against the hard ground, jarring the pistol from his hand. It slid across the ground, came to rest just out of reach.

Bolt glanced down at Cripps when he rode by him, still in pursuit of the other gunman. Cripps writhed in pain, clutching his bloody chest. Blood oozed across his fingers, splattered his clothing. He tried to curse Bolt, but he had no voice. Pink foam frothed from the corner of his mouth and Bolt knew he had taken the bullet in the lungs. He was still alive, but he wouldn't last long.

Turner spun around in his saddle, looked back to see who had been hit. He saw Bolt coming up fast behind him. He took quick aim, squeezed the trigger.

A second later, Bolt heard Amylou scream as Turner's bullet struck her leg. Turner's careless shot had missed Bolt, hit her instead. The bullet went clean through the fleshy part of her thigh. She staggered backwards, tumbled to the ground, landed on her back. She raised her head to look down at her wound, clamped her hand over it quickly to stem the flow of blood that spurted from the hole. A black cloud fogged her brain as she fell into unconsciousness.

Bolt turned his head, saw Amylou on the ground, blood spreading across her riding breeches. She was motionless and Bolt couldn't tell if she was still alive.

"You dirty bastard!" he yelled at Turner.

Turner took aim again.

Bolt was quicker. He fired a rapid shot at Turner, aiming for his shooting arm. The hit was dead on.

Turner's arm jerked straight out from his body as he tried to shake off the pain that seared through his upper arm. His fingers opened automatically, releasing their grip on the pistol. It dropped to the ground, was mashed into the dirt when the horse trampled across it.

Bolt followed his advantage, moved on in. He took aim again but didn't shoot. He wanted information and he was in a position to get it.

As Turner grabbed his arm with his other hand, he looked in Bolt's direction, saw that Bolt was still after him. Turner ducked down, then slipped off his horse on the side away from Bolt. He planned to use his horse for cover, but the horse kept going. He tried desperately to hold on to the saddlehorn and move with the horse, but with only one good arm, his other hand finally slipped off the horn. As he lost his grip, he was thrown off balance. He staggered back, tripped over his own feet. He crashed

83

to the ground, landed just ten yards from the spot where Cripps lay dying in a pool of blood.

Bolt rode up to Turner, quickly dismounted, his pistol cocked. He walked over to Turner, aimed the pistol between the man's eyes.

"Where's Bascomb?" Bolt asked, easing his finger around the trigger.

Turner stared up at him with a mean, cold look in his eyes.

"None of your fucking business," he said defiantly. "I ain't tellin' you anything."

"You got a choice, stranger. You tell me where Bascomb is or I make coyote meat out of you."

"He's at Eagle Lake."

"Where's that?"

"South of here."

"Then he's with the bunch that went the other way. Right?" Bolt started to pull the trigger when Turner hesitated.

"Yes." Turner's voice began to tremble.

"Who set up Amylou? Miss Lovett?"

Bolt saw movement out of the corner of his eye. He looked over just in time to see Cripps retrieve his pistol from the dirt, bring it up and aim it. He aimed at Turner.

Bolt turned, took aim.

He fired at the same time Cripps did.

Cripps slumped back to the ground, dead on the spot.

Bolt turned back to Turner. His stomach turned queasy and he fought down the bile that rose in his throat.

Turner's face was blown away. Chunks of flesh and brain matter splattered on the dirt around him.

Turner would not be the one to tell him who the inside

man, or woman, was who helped arrange the robbery.

Bolt ran back to Amylou. He crouched down, leaned over her, looked for signs of life. He saw her chest move up and down slowly in the slow rhythm of breathing.

"Amylou! Amylou!" He patted her cheeks, called her name again.

Her eyes fluttered open. She looked up at him, tried to get her bearings.

"Are you all right, Bolt?" she said, her voice weak and low. Her thigh wound was numb and she felt no pain.

"I'm O.K., but you've got a pretty nasty wound. Were you hit anyplace besides your leg?"

Then she remembered that she had been hit. She sat up, looked down at her bloody clothes. Her head began to swim in darkness and she struggled to remain conscious.

"No, I don't think I'm hurt anyplace else. How bad is it?"

"Pretty bad. You've lost a lot of blood."

"What about the other two?"

"Both dead." He didn't want Amylou to see how they died.

He checked her to be sure she had not been hit anyplace other than the leg. Then he eased her back to the ground.

"Just stay put until I check your leg."

He reached his hand around to the underside of her leg, felt the sticky blood that oozed from the exit wound. He was grateful that the bullet had gone clear through, but he had to stop the bleeding right away.

He dashed over to his horse which was close by, opened a saddlebag and fished through it. He drew out a strip of cloth, took it back to Amylou. He tied the cloth around her pants, just above the wound. He tightened it, tied a knot.

"Think you can ride?" he asked.

"Yes," she said, her voice weak.

Bolt knew she could not ride very far. She had lost too much blood and was too weak.

He had a decision to make. He wanted to ride on to Eagle Lake, find Bascomb before he found out about the two dead men, but he knew Amylou couldn't make the trip. She needed medical attention right away. He'd have to go on into Etinger.

He knew he still faced three men in Etinger. Three men waiting to kill him if he showed up. He was surprised that no one from the town had ridden out to check on the gunfire, but maybe in a town like Etinger, they were so used to shootings that they didn't pay any attention to them. Or maybe no one had heard the shots.

He looked up at the sky. With the clouds still above them, it would get dark early tonight. It was already beginning to darken and it would be totally dark in another half hour. It would be safer to wait, go into the town after dark.

He helped Amylou to a sitting position, then very carefully, picked her up in his arms. He knew he couldn't wait out in the open. He looked around for a place to stay until dark. When he saw the weathered stagecoach, he knew that would give them the cover they needed. He carried her over to the coach, walked around behind it and set her down on the ground.

"I'll round up our horses and be right back," he told her.

A few minutes later, he was back, leading the two horses by the reins. He looped the reins around a slab of wood that jutted out on the backside of the coach, then returned to Amylou.

As soon as he felt it was dark enough, he helped her up in her saddle, told her to ride slow. He checked her wound in the darkness, with his fingers. The bleeding had stopped.

Instead of riding right into main street, and possibly a trap, he decided to circle around the town, come in from the back.

He stopped at the first house that he saw that had lights glowing inside. The house was set back away from the town.

An elderly gentleman answered his knock.

"Is there a doctor in town?" Bolt asked. "I have a sick lady out here."

"We ain't got a doctor here."

Bolt's heart sank.

"Who takes care of your sick?"

"Tell you what you do, stranger," the man said as he spit a wad of tobacco out the door. "You take your lady friend to Miss Gaines' house. She'll take care of her."

"Where does Miss Gaines live?"

"Over yonder. See those lights down there. That's her house. She's a widow lady, nice as can be. Young, too, to be a widow. Only twenty-four, or is it twenty-five now. Yes sir, she's a midwife and a damned good nurse."

"Thank you, sir," Bolt said, backing away before the old man could tell him Miss Gaines' whole history.

Chapter Nine

Red Harrington made it a nightly ritual to stop at the Red River Saloon after he had finished cooking at his small cafe next door. His good-natured wife, Kathleen, always shooed him out of the restaurant after he had helped sweep up, wash the tables off. She always refused his offer to help with the dishes, saying that when she wanted her fine china broken, she'd let him know.

The Harringtons were a friendly couple and well-liked by everyone in town. They had lost their only baby when it was less than a year old and Mrs. Harrington was never able to have another child. So their restaurant business gave them the opportunity to keep in touch with people which helped to relieve their loneliness, their profound sadness at not being able to have children.

Mr. Harrington was pleased that his wife would not let him help with the dishes. He enjoyed the time he spent at the Red River Saloon talking to the people. It gave him a chance to catch up with the town's gossip which he shared with his wife when they returned to their house. He knew, in fact, that one of the reasons Kathleen kicked him out at the same time every night was so that he could learn the things that people didn't talk about in a cafe.

He particularly liked to talk to Loretta Sweeney. He had a special rapport with her, a closeness that she didn't seem to share with anyone else. Maybe it was her red hair, like his own, that made their friendship so unique, but he knew it went deeper than that. He read the sadness in her eyes, the sadness that went deeper than her rather harsh face. He related it to his own sadness about the death of his baby daughter. Even though it had been more than twenty-five years since his little girl had died, it was something that he never got over. It was something that he and his wife did not talk about anymore, but sometimes, at odd moments, he saw the same sadness in Kathleen's eyes.

When Harrington had first met Loretta, the sight of her red hair had stirred the memories of his lost little baby. He had begun playing a little game with himself, pretending that Loretta was his little girl, all grown up. The pretending had gone on so long, it seemed like a reality to him now. He thought of Loretta as his own daughter. She even called him "Pops," when everyone else called him "Red." The fact that Loretta's background was mysterious, a well-guarded secret, made it even easier for Harrington to identify with her. He could give her any background he wished. And the background he preferred was that she was kidnapped from her parents when she was young, raised by poor people, leaving home to make it on her own.

Harrington never had more than one drink at the saloon and he always left after listening to Loretta sing a song, when she would stop by his table and talk to him before she had to sing again.

Tom had joined Harrington at Red's favorite table tonight. He was watching the saloon as Bolt had asked him to. Keeping an eye on the employees to see if anything funny was going on or if one of them disappeared. Tess Hummer didn't like the noise and business of the saloon at night so she chose to stay in their room upstairs, the room where they had settled after moving from the Sundowners Hotel following the robbery.

Tess had spent some time with Tom in the saloon earlier that day and evening. She had noticed his mild flirtations with the glitter gals, the way he looked at Loretta Sweeney. But she paid little attention to it. It was a man's nature to have a roving eye when it came to pretty girls. As long as he didn't get too friendly, she didn't mind. She knew it was important for Tom to keep his eye on the saloon. She understood the suspicions about Amylou's employees and she felt very uncomfortable around any of them.

Right now, Tom had his eyes on Loretta, watching her as she sang a sad ballad, talking to Red Harrington between songs. The fact that he was watching her had nothing to do with Bolt's instructions. Even though she was quite a bit older than he was, he was fascinated by her. There was something earthy about her that intrigued him, something sensual about her lips when she sang or smiled, something that stirred him about her svelte body when she walked.

Loretta finished her song, smiled and nodded her head to the spontaneous applause. Tom watched her as she strolled toward their table. He noticed how her creamy white breasts jutted up above the low neckline of her green taffeta dress. Desire loomed in his loins as she walked toward the table, her long narrow skirt hugging the crevice of her sex.

"Hi, Pops," she greeted the older man, "see you got out of doing the dishes again." She patted him on the head affectionately, ruffled up the strands of red hair. It was a ritual with her.

"Nice song. I'm proud of you, me lass."

"Would you like a drink, Loretta?" Tom offered. He wondered what the hell Harrington had to be proud of. Red wasn't Loretta's father.

"A sarsaparilla would be nice," she said, barely noticing Tom.

Tom waved for Carl Anders. When the bartender came to the table, Tom ordered the sarsaparilla, another whiskey for himself. Harrington refused a second drink. When Anders delivered the drinks a few minutes later, Tom dug in his pants pocket, drew out a dollar bill and placed it on Anders' tray. Something dark and soft slipped out of his pocket when he pulled the money out. It fell to the floor near his chair, making no sound when it hit. Tom didn't notice it.

Bored by, or perhaps envious of, the exchange of conversation between the singer and the older Irishman, Tom fulfilled his obligation to Bolt by watching the bartender and Cole Megan, the poker dealer, for a while. He saw nothing erratic in either one of their behavior patterns, even though he didn't particularly like either one of them. He wanted to put the boots to Loretta and he hadn't been able to get to first base with her yet. He was glad when he heard Harrington announce that he must get back to his waiting wife.

"Goodbye, Pops," Loretta said. "See you tomorrow night."

When Harrington rose from his chair, he spotted something dark on the floor, near Tom's chair. He stooped over, picked it up. When he saw what it was, he held it out from his body with his thumb and forefinger.

"This dirty sock belong to you, Tom?" he asked.

Tom's heart skipped a beat when he saw it. That was Bolt's sock. The one that contained all of Bolt's cash, close to three thousand. That was the second time that day he'd lost the sock. The first time was when he'd forgotten it and left it in his room at the Sundowners Hotel when he and Tess moved over to the saloon. Shit, he had to be more careful of it. Bolt would string him up by the balls if he lost it.

"Yair, thanks," He took the sock from Harrington.

"Odd thing for a man to carry around. What's in it, your handkerchief?" Harrington laughed.

Tom looked at the sock, saw its bulge.

"No," he grinned. "Actually, it's the matching sock. You see, I have a tendency to misplace the mates to my socks, so I always stick one inside of the other." He glanced over at Loretta, saw her staring at the sock. He didn't think he was fooling her, but she said nothing.

Harrington smiled and shook his head, thinking the young man a wee bit eccentric. He said goodbye and left Loretta and Tom alone at the table.

Tom was just about to strike up a conversation with the sensual singer when she rose from the table.

"Time for me to sing another song," she said, her husky voice sending chills of desire down Tom's back, around to his groin. "It's been nice talking to you, Tom."

What talking? Tom wondered. The only words the two of them had exchanged was when Tom offered to buy her a drink and she accepted.

Frustrated, Tom went upstairs to his room.

Tess was waiting in bed for him when he got there, stark naked under the covers.

"You through flirting with all the girls so soon?" she teased.

"Yep," he grinned. "They all wanted to ravage my beautiful body. I had to come up here to escape them. If anybody knocks, don't let them in."

Tess grabbed a pillow, heaved it at Tom.

"Oh, Tom, you nut," she laughed. "Why is it men think they're so irresistible that all girls will simply swoon if they can't have them?" She swung her arm out in an exaggerated gesture.

"Because we *are* irresistible." He hooked his thumbs into his armpits, strutted across to the bed and leered at her.

"Come here, then," she cooed, "and let me ravage your body."

Before he stripped out of his clothes, Tom stuffed Bolt's dark blue money sock under the mattress, where it would be safe.

"Don't dare lose this," he said, shoving it as far as he could.

"You're lucky someone didn't steal it when you left it at the hotel this morning."

"Damned lucky." A twinge of pain stabbed at his loins when he thought what Bolt would do to him if he lost that money.

He climbed in next to Tess' warm soft body.

His manhood was already stiff and pulsing with desire. He knew that when he made love to Tess tonight, he would be thinking of someone else.

He couldn't get Loretta Sweeney out of his mind.

Amylou was weak, about to pass out by the time they reached the house. She hunched forward in the saddle, leaned her head on her arm, which was draped across the front part of the saddle.

Bolt had ridden at a slow pace, watching her as he rode on his own horse. He held the reins to Amylou's horse in

93

his hands, led the animal so that it rode alongside his own horse.

When he reached the house, he dismounted, tied both horses to a fence post, then lifted Amylou down gently from her saddle. She was light and lifeless in his arms as he carried her to the door.

Bolt tapped on the bottom of the door with the toe of his boot.

"Miss Gaines!" he called, "Are you in there?"

He heard the shuffle of footsteps beyond the door.

"Who is it?" called the woman's voice.

"The name's Bolt. I've got a sick girl out here who needs your help!"

Constance Gaines opened the door immediately. The light from her house threw a shaft of light on the strangers at her door. She saw the blood on Amylou's riding pants, the bloody rag tied around the wound.

"Oh, my," she said. "Bring her inside." She stepped aside to allow Bolt to enter her house with the sick girl. She picked up one of the lanterns from the living room, led Bolt to the front bedroom. "Just set her down on the bed."

Bolt waited for Miss Gaines to throw back the covers before he lowered Amylou to the bed.

Amylou's eyes fluttered, then she looked up at Bolt with searching eyes.

"Am I going to make it?" she asked, her voice barely audible.

"Of course you are," Bolt reassured her. "Miss Gaines is going to take care of you."

"Constance Gaines. Please call me Connie," the young woman said, her words crisp and cool, a tone of efficiency in her voice. She placed the lantern on a table near the bed, leaned over to examine Amylou's leg wound.

94

Because of the long pants Amylou wore, she couldn't tell much about the wound, but at first glance it looked like a bullet hole.

Amylou tried to raise her head to look at her leg. Bolt pushed her back down.

"Just relax, Amylou," he soothed.

Connie turned away, walked to the dresser where she picked up a tray of medical supplies.

"Has the girl been shot?" Connie asked without turning her head around to look at Bolt. "Is that a bullet wound?" Again her words were crisp, unaccusing.

"Yes," said Bolt. "Seems like there are some unfriendly types around."

"I understand," was all she said.

Bolt watched Connie as she worked quickly, cutting the pants leg away. Her light brown hair was pulled back away from her face, fastened in a severe bun at the back of her head. Her long dress was plain, but it did not hide her full figure.

"The bleeding has stopped, which is a good sign. Did she lose much blood?"

"Quite a bit," Bolt said.

Connie took a swatch of cotton from the tray, dipped it in a jar of sterilized water, then dabbed around the edges of the wound. She leaned down, examined the underside of the leg, found the spot where the bullet had exited.

Amylou winced in pain as Connie touched the tender skin.

"You're very fortunate, Amylou," she said, her voice softening. "The bullet passed on through your leg. I'll clean the wound and bandage it."

"Will it hurt?" Amylou asked, her soft voice trembling.

"Yes, it will hurt, but I will give you some elixir so the

95

pain will not be unbearable." She reached over to the tray, poured a small glass full of a brown fluid from a bottle labeled simply "Elixir." The fluid was mostly whiskey, alcohol, with a little flavoring thrown in to alter the taste of it.

Bolt raised Amylou to a half-sitting position, helped Connie administer the medicine to the sick girl.

Amylou drank it slowly, wrinkling her nose at the strong taste of the medicine.

"I'll have to remove her pants," Connie said. "Can you help me, Mister Bolt?"

"Drop the 'mister.' It's just Bolt."

He lifted Amylou's hips in the air as Connie slid the long pants carefully down her legs. She set the bloodied pants on the dresser as Bolt lowered Amylou to the bed.

"It will take a few minutes for the medicine to take effect. Would you like to sit down, Bolt?" Connie walked to the far corner of the room, sat down in one of the straightback chairs, offered the other one to Bolt.

"She won't be able to be moved tonight," Connie said. "You are both welcome to stay here. I have plenty of room, four bedrooms, in fact. I'm used to this, so don't think you're causing any imposition."

"I appreciate it. When you're through with Amylou, I have some business in town I have to take care of, but I'll be back and take you up on your offer. It's been a long day."

Bolt noticed the way Connie was studying him, as if she was trying to decide whether he was the good guy or the bad.

"Anything I can help you with?" she asked, her blue eyes now soft and gentle.

"Maybe. I'm looking for three men. Know where I

might find them?"

"Are they on the dodge?"

"Sort of. If they aren't now, they soon will be. Yes, they're on the dodge. They're part of the Bascomb bunch. You know him?"

Bolt saw her shudder when he mentioned Bascomb's name.

"Yes, I know who he is. That who shot your friend?"

"One of his men."

"I hope you killed him."

"I did. Two of them. But there are three more of them here in Etinger."

"Men like that always hang out at Bill's Card Parlor and Saloon, but it's a dangerous place to go. Guns are always going off in there. Men who don't make it are buried in the woods without grave markers. You'd be better off staying here, ride out in the morning."

"With two dead bodies out in the road just outside of town? It won't be long before they're combing the town for me. I have to face them down before they come looking for me. It might give me a little advantage that way. I'll need all the help I can get."

She rose from her chair, walked back over to the bed.

"You're right. You wouldn't be safe here with them on the loose. Especially if they know your friend is wounded."

"I don't think any of them know that Amylou is with me."

"Even so, if you were in a shootout, they might figure you were hurt. This is the first place they'd look."

"That sort of puts you in danger too, doesn't it?"

"Not really. I treat both sides, the good and the bad. When someone's brought in here hurt or wounded, I don't look too close to see which side they're on. Besides, it's not my place to judge another person. My job is to take care of sick people, make them well, if I can. The outlaws know how I feel and they come here for help as often as anyone else. They wouldn't harm me."

Bolt admired her for her honesty, her philosophy. He found himself again wishing that there did not have to be bad and good in this world.

"How are you feeling?" Connie asked Amylou.

Amylou looked up at her with droopy, bleary eyes. She tried to answer but her words were slurred beyond recognition. She closed her eyes again, her mind drifting away in a mindless fog.

"Hold her leg down while I clean the wound. She'll still feel the pain."

Bolt placed his palms on Amylou's bare legs, applied a gentle pressure.

Connie worked quickly, dabbing blood from the skin. She poured a cleansing fluid into the wound. Amylou's leg jerked as the sleeping girl tried to move away from the dull pain that floated in her brain, piercing the fog of oblivion.

When she was finished wrapping a bandage around the leg, she picked up the lantern, walked out of the room.

"Don't worry about her. She'll probably sleep all night. I'll leave the door unlocked, but I'll be awake anyway."

"Thanks," said Bolt, so grateful he wanted to take the nurse in his arms and hug her. Instead he walked out into the darkness.

He was ready to face the enemy.

Chapter Ten

The sound of loud voices, filthy language and raucous laughter rang out from the saloon at the far end of town.

Bolt heard it from a block away. He rode close enough to look at the sign: Bill's Card Parlor & Saloon. The saloon was located at the opposite end of town from where he and Amylou had been involved in the shootout. With all that noise inside the saloon, it was no wonder no one heard the gun shots or came to check on them. Evidently the first two men were to take him out and the other three men weren't concerned enough to make sure the job was done.

A small dirt road joined the main street on the corner where the saloon was situated. Bolt studied the escape paths, decided to tie Nick up around the corner from the front of the saloon, near the side dirt road. He didn't want Nick right outside the saloon entrance, just in case anyone recognized the horse. And by parking him at the side of the building, he would have a straight shot back to Connie's place if he needed it.

He rode around the corner, dismounted, looped the reins around the side hitchrail. He checked his pistol, walked around to the front of the building. He paused, took a deep breath, then pushed the batwing doors open.

The room was even noisier inside. The harsh sounds crashed in around him, made him want to cover up his ears. Only a few men glanced up at him as he came through the door.

Pausing just inside the doorway, Bolt scanned the room quickly, taking in all the faces that he could see. All of the customers looked like hardcases, drifters, riders of the hoot-owl trail, outlaws. Any one of the customers could be the ones he was looking for. That's where he had the disadvantage. He didn't know who they were, what they looked like, but chances were, they would be able to spot him immediately. All he had to go on was one name, Jake. And he wasn't sure Jake was with the group that rode into Etinger.

As he walked toward the long bar, he noticed that two men at the far end of the bar were still watching him. Muscles began to ripple underneath his skin. He hooked his thumbs into his waistband where he could draw in a hurry if need be.

He strode to the short end of the long bar, stood facing the two men at the opposite end. He glanced at them, tried to make out something familiar about them.

The bartender, a tall, stoop-shouldered man, stepped up to Bolt, briefly blocking Bolt's view of the two men. The bartender said nothing, tapped his knuckles on the counter in front of him and waited for Bolt to order.

"Whiskey. Short and sweet," Bolt said.

The bartender grabbed a bottle from the back shelf, poured a healthy slug into a small glass, shoved it toward Bolt. Digging into his pocket, Bolt fished out the coins to pay for the drink, slapped them on the counter. When the bartender moved away, Bolt glanced down at the far end of the bar. The two men were turned, talking to each other. The loud din of the bar made it impossible for Bolt to hear what they were saying.

He took a sip of his drink, holding the glass tumbler in

his left hand. His other hand stayed close to his pistol.

The man on the left glanced up at Bolt, his pale blue eyes cold as ice. There was something familiar about the eyes, but Bolt couldn't be sure.

The other man moved his left hand down, below the level of the counter top.

Bolt eased his hand over so it touched the butt of his pistol. He watched. Waited. Ready. His muscles tensed as the man's hand. Bolt saw the flash of metal, started to draw before he realized the man did not have a gun in his hand. Bolt eased the pistol back into the holster.

Hoke Talley, the left-handed man, held a metal key up in his hand, tossed it down the bar.

"This yours?" he laughed.

The key slid down the length of the bar top, came to rest a few inches in front of Bolt. He recognized it as the key to his hotel room in Houston. He also noticed the wheezing voice of the man who had worn a bandanna over his face the last time Bolt had seen him.

Bolt reached for the key, started to pick it up.

The other man, Whit Stoneman, stepped away from the bar, his hand hovering above his pistol butt.

Bolt recognized Stoneman, then, but didn't know his name. The leather wrist bands, the matching pair of six-guns, the hand-carved pistol grips of the holstered pistols, the blonde shaggy hair.

"It'll cost you fifty bucks for that key," Stoneman said. "That's what Bascomb paid for it."

Sensing trouble, the other customers at the bar began to move back, their eyes darting back and forth, from one end of the bar to the other, as if they were watching a tennis game.

Bolt moved his hand away from the key, looked at

Stoneman, his eyes unflinching.

"Where's your friend?" Bolt said, his calm voice echoing out in the still room.

"Who're you talking about?" Stoneman snarled.

"Jake."

"Jake rode on through."

Bolt noticed the other men in the room as his eyes darted around. He felt they were neutral, but he knew if he made even one mistake, he'd buy it, one way or the other. Stoneman and Talley seemed to be known here at the saloon.

Bolt saw the movement out of the corner of his eye. His eyes shot over to the bar. The bartender was starting to reach under the counter.

"Back away from there," Bolt warned. "This trouble is between me and those two jaspers. You reach under that counter and it becomes your trouble, too."

The bartender raised his hands in the air, stepped back against the wall.

But the other men in the room stiffened, fanned out even farther as hands started moving toward holstered pistols.

The room became deadly quiet.

"Is it one against all here?" Bolt asked, his voice booming out into the stillness. "Or does a man get a chance to pay his own way?"

A man at a nearby table spoke up.

"You handle them two, and you'll walk out of here under your own power."

"Yeah," said another. "But you're easy pickin's, stranger. Them men are fast. You stand up against them two and you got a free ticket home."

Stoneman went for it.

Bolt saw the movement the instant Stoneman's hand began to move toward his pistol.

Bolt's hand flew to his pistol, brought it up, cocked on the upswing. He fired before Stoneman could clear leather.

Bolt's bullet walloped into Stoneman's chest, exploded his heart.

Stoneman's eyes widened in surprise, just before he crashed over backwards, dead before he hit the floor.

The customers gasped, moved back even farther.

Hoke Talley brought up his pistol in his left hand. It was already drawn and cocked. He fired pointblank at Bolt at the same instant Bolt whirled and shot at him.

Bolt's shot was another heart shot. Talley gasped, clutched at his chest as he stumbled backwards. He drew his hands away from his chest, stared down at them. He sucked in a breath as he saw the blood that covered them dripped down his wrists. It was the last breath he took as he crumbled to the floor, dead, his body piled on top of Stoneman's.

Bolt's body stiffened for a brief instant as he took the impact of Talley's bullet. He caught his breath, looked around the room to see if there were any more takers.

No one moved, except to look in the direction of the two dead men.

Bolt holstered his pistol, stepped back to the bar.

Men started talking about the shooting, arguing whether Bolt had been hit or not. Some swore Talley's shot was straight on. Others said no, the stranger was still alive.

Bolt picked up his key, stuffed it in his pocket. He picked up his drink, downed it in one gulp.

Trying to restore some semblance of order, the

bartender called out. "Next drink's on the house, gentlemen!"

The customers migrated toward the bar, having a new story to tell their friends.

Bolt reached in his pocket, pulled out a twenty-dollar bill. He plunked it down on the bar as the bartender approached him.

"For their burials," he said tightly. "Decent or indecent, I don't give a damn."

"You care for another drink?" the bartender asked as he took the twenty.

"No. But if you're calling the undertaker, tell him there's two more just like those on the road, just outside of town."

He turned and walked across the saloon floor, out the batwing doors.

The men inside were still debating whether Bolt had been shot or not.

He walked slowly to the corner of the building. The minute he rounded the corner, he doubled over in pain. Talley's bullet had hit his belt buckle and splintered. He ran his finger across the buckle, felt the small dent on the surface of the thick metal. He ran his hand down to his left hip where the pain was so bad. When he touched it he knew that a small fragment of the lead had pierced his flesh.

He leaned against the wall, steadied himself as his head began to swim in darkness. He took a deep breath, kept himself alert.

Using the wall for a prop, he moved slowly toward his horse. Each step he took brought a surge of pain through his hip.

He pulled himself up in the saddle but the pain was so

intense when he moved his leg, he could not swing it across the horse.

Riding side-saddle, he made it back to Connie's house.

Connie heard the hoofbeats approaching. She had the door open for him when he rode clear up to the steps and slipped down from his horse.

"You ride side-saddle?" she laughed when she saw him. It wasn't until he stepped inside the house that she realized that he was hurt. She saw the dark red circle that stained the side of his trousers.

"Yeah, it's a new trick I just learned," he said.

"Bolt, you've been shot! Does it hurt?"

"Only when I walk."

"Let's get a look at it. Come on in the bedroom."

Connie helped him to the back bedroom. The pain had subsided, but every time he moved the one leg to take a step, it felt like a knife pierced him.

"How's Amylou?" he asked when they got to the bedroom.

"She's doing fine. She's still asleep, but she's breathing normally and she has no fever."

"Will she be all right?"

"She may limp for a few days, but if she takes it easy, she'll be all right."

"We'll make quite a pair. Both of us limping."

Connie lit the lantern in the bedroom, looked at him.

"O.K. Let's get those trousers off."

Bolt gave her a funny look, suddenly embarrassed. "Now?"

"Why, Mister Bolt, you're not shy are you?"

She stepped up to him, began unbuttoning the front of his pants.

He stepped back.

"I can do it." He removed his gunbelt, handed it to her, then eased the trousers down over his hips, pulled them off his feet.

Connie set the pistol on the dresser, walked back to Bolt.

"Now the shorts," she said.

"Do I have to?"

"How else am I going to look at your wound. I'm a nurse, remember?"

Bolt slipped the shorts down, let them fall to the floor. He eased himself down on the bed. Connie helped him lift his legs onto the bed, propped a pillow under his head.

Stretched out on the bed, naked from the waist down, Bolt didn't know why he felt so self-conscious. He'd been naked in front of a woman before. Plenty of times. But this time it was different. Maybe it was because he felt helpless instead of powerful. Or maybe it was because he realized how attractive Connie was as she hovered close above him.

Connie examined the wound, saw the small sliver of lead that had lodged in his flesh about a half inch deep. It was high in his hip, in the flesh part. She quickly determined that no bone had been hit by the fragment of bullet. She pressed her fingers in various spots around his hip, his stomach, the other hip, testing for soreness that would indicate that another piece of lead had penetrated his body. She tested his upper legs next, pushing against the skin with both hands, then moving to another spot to do the same.

When her hands touched his inner thighs, he felt a surge of desire flood his loins.

"Don't stop," he joked, trying to ease his own embarrassment.

She noticed his manhood begin to stiffen, but she moved her hand away, kept an air of professionalism about her.

"There's just one small sliver of lead embedded in your flesh. It should be easy to remove. Do you want some elixir?"

"No. Just go for it."

Connie stepped over to the dresser, picked up the things she needed to remove the piece of lead.

"Oooooooohh!" Bolt cried when she dabbed the wound with alcohol.

She picked up an instrument that looked like a long pair of tweezers. In her other hand, she held a piece of alcohol-soaked cotton.

"Now hang on. It'll just take a minute to get this out."

Bolt reached up and grabbed the bedposts. He thought he would come right up off the bed when she probed in his flesh with the tweezers. His knuckles became white as he gripped the posts with all his might.

"Shiiiiiiiitt!" he screamed when she wrapped the tweezers around the lead sliver and extracted it. She dabbed the cotton across the raw wound once more, then announced that it was all over.

"That wasn't so bad, was it? I'll put a bandage on it and you'll be good as new."

Bolt brought his hands down from the bedpost, glad that she was through. He relaxed as she prepared a small bandage.

When she applied the bandage, her arm brushed across his bare manhood. The contrast between the pain and the gentle brush of her arm was excruciating. His cock twitched, began to grow. Her hand touched him again. This time it lingered, pressed against his growing shaft.

Bolt felt more helpless than he had before. There was nothing he could do about his swelling member. But now he didn't care. Her delicate touch excited him beyond all reason.

Connie glanced down at the swollen mass, wrapped her hand around it, moved her hand slowly up and down its length.

"Don't stop," he husked again. Only this time he meant it.

"I won't."

Chapter Eleven

It was already dark when Jake Putnam woke from his nap. He sat up, stretched his muscles, scooted his tall, muscular frame over to the edge of the bed, fumbled in the dark for the coal oil lamp, the matches to light it.

Evidently, the man they were waiting for hadn't shown up. Otherwise, he would have been awakened so he could ride on back to Eagle Lake to report to Ord Bascomb. He and the other four men who worked for Bascomb had agreed to sleep in shifts so that at least two men were stationed just outside of town at all times.

Bascomb had been so sure that Bolt would choose the trail that led to Etinger. And Jake had seen how spunky the girl had been. It wouldn't surprise him at all if the Lovett girl hadn't come with him.

Bascomb had told the men that there'd be no posse chasin' them down. At least not a posse headed by Connors, the sheriff. Miss Lovett would get no help there. If there was a posse, it would have to be formed by the girl and Bolt.

Putnam reached for his gunbelt that hung on the bed poster, slipped it around his waist and fastened it. He had slept in his clothes in case he had been called out while he slept. He picked up a boot, stuck his toes inside, then pulled it up over his foot. He picked up the other boot, tugged at it to get it on. That boot was always harder to get on.

He walked over to the dresser, poured water from the porcelain pitcher into the bowl. He dipped his hands into the water, splashed it on his face. He glanced up in the mirror, traced a finger across the long scar on his left cheek that ran from the corner of his eye clear down to his jaw.

He resented the scar, what it represented. Jake had been Bascomb's right hand man at one time. But Bascomb had demoted him to just one of the boys right after he got the scar. It wasn't the scar itself. Hell, Billings' face was more beat up than his. Billings couldn't even open his eye all the way, and his nose looked like it had been cut off, smashed by a hammer, then glued back on. Yet Bascomb had appointed Randy Billings as second in command after Jake had gotten his face carved up.

Bascomb had blamed Jake for the foul up of that stage robbery, but it had been as much Billings' fault as anyone elses. But Bascomb didn't see it that way. Jake's only problem was that he had allowed the stage driver to get close enough to slice a knife across his face. So now Randy Billings was sitting pretty down in Eagle Lake, pampered by Bascomb, gettin' the easy jobs. He hated Billings with a passion. Billings was probably bedded down with some whore by now while he still faced the long ride to Eagle Lake to make his report. He hoped to hell that Bolt had stopped to sleep someplace. Jake didn't fancy making that long ride in the dark.

Jake wondered what time it was, how long he'd slept. He walked over to the window in his hotel room, threw open the window. Bill's Saloon across the street was going full blast by the sound of it, so it must be way past supper time. There was always a lull in the activity when some of the customers stopped to eat.

Jake blew out the lantern, left the room, walked across the street to the saloon. Inside, he scanned the room, looking for Whit Stoneman and Hoke Talley. He didn't see them. He walked to the far end of the bar where there was room for a man to stand. That's when he saw the dark stain on the floor. A pang of horror struck him as he stared down at it. No, it couldn't have been his partners in the robbery. Bolt wouldn't have gotten this far. He was to be taken out on the trail back there, before he got to town.

Jake stepped around the stain on the floor, edged up to the bar. Hell, there were shootings all the time in this bar, so there was nothing to worry about. Some drunks just didn't know how to handle their liquor.

"You lookin' fer yer friends?" asked the man on his right.

"Yeah. You seen 'em?" Jake asked.

The man nodded toward the fresh stain on the floor. "They bought it. About an hour ago."

Jake was stunned.

"How'd it happen?"

"Some stranger came in here about an hour ago and blasted them away. Must have been somebody they knowed 'cause Talley tossed a key to him. That's when all the trouble started."

Jake couldn't believe what he was hearing. How could one man take out Talley and Stoneman who were two of the fastest guns he knew.

The bartender walked over to Jake, didn't smile.

"Sorry about your friends, Putnam," Walt, the bartender said. "I'll buy you a drink. Want whiskey?"

"Yes," said Jake, trying to sort things out in his mind.

Walt set a glass down in front of Jake, poured it full.

111

"Walt, have you seen either Cripps or Turner this evening?"

"They . . . they're dead, too."

"What?" Jake's head spun with the news.

"Yeah," said Walt. "After the stranger had killed your friends, he told me there were two more bodies out on the trail. When the undertaker was through here, he went for the other two. He stopped by a few minutes ago, told me who they were."

"Was the stranger wounded?" Jake asked.

"Nope," said Walt. "He walked out of here standing up."

"Oh yes he was," said the man on Jake's right. "I saw his body jerk when he caught Talley's bullet."

"No. He wasn't hit," offered another man. "He never flinched once."

And the argument was on again.

Jake thought about it for a minute. He downed the drink in one gulp.

If Bolt had been wounded, Jake knew just where to look for him. There was only one place in town where a man could get medical attention.

Bolt felt only a dull ache where the bullet fragment had been imbedded in his flesh. The searing pain had gone away the minute Connie had removed it. But he didn't care about that anymore. The pleasure he felt right then was too exquisite.

Connie's warm mouth sheathed his cock in a fiery bath of pure ecstasy. She hunched over his loins, her smooth bare legs straddling his. Her hot hand gripped the base of his cock as she bobbed her head up and down, swathing his swollen mass in frothy spittle.

112

He felt as though he were a fine instrument being played by a virtuoso. Her suckling mouth at his cock, her delicate fingers on his flesh sparked unseen fires, tuned him up for the performance to follow. Her free hand roamed his body, traced a delicate path across his tummy, his inner thighs. His flesh tingled like a harp everywhere her hand traveled, plucking arpeggios from the fine hairs that covered his body.

He looked down at her in the soft glow of light from the lantern, saw only the top of her head, the ashen brown hair, released from its tight bun, flowing down around her face. He reached down, ran his fingers through the silken hair, then pressed her head down into his crotch.

She suckled him even harder, her cheeks caving in from the exertion. She lapped at the flared tip of his cock, her tongue rough and stiff against the delicate flesh.

She backed away, finally, gripping his shaft with firm lips until she pulled it all the way out. The air engulfed his damp, sensitive cock like a gentle spring shower, sending a tingling ripple of pleasure across his body.

She looked up at him, starry-eyed from the passion that coursed through her own hungry loins.

"You're so big. So hard," she husked.

Her words washed over him like a soothing balm.

She moved up his body, kissed him with hot, damp lips. He tasted the lemony flavor of his own sex on her lips. Her tongue darted into his mouth in search of a playmate. Its stiffness found his tongue, rubbed against it, circled it, darted in and out of his mouth.

He wanted to tip her over on the bed, plunge her depths with his own probe. He wanted to feel her lower lips wrap around his cock as her other ones had. He wanted her to take his shaft deep inside her, hold it there

113

with her warmth.

He pushed against her shoulders, but she did not move back.

Instead, she positioned herself above him, hovered like a hummingbird in search of sweet nectar. Grasping the base of his cock with one hand, she lowered herself to him, guided him to the slit of her sex lips.

He shuddered with tingling shoots of pleasure as she dropped down, smothering his pulsing mass with the soft damp folds of her sex. She rocked back and forth on his cock as if she were riding bareback on a stallion.

The pain in his hip was gone, numbed by the intense pleasure he felt in his groin.

He thrust his loins up to meet her as she assaulted him with her bobbing sex. He felt her body shudder in the throes of orgasm.

He rolled her over on her back, never losing contact with her throbbing sheath. He moved his legs around, straddled her wide-spread legs. He withdrew his cock, clear to the tip, then rammed it home, plummeting her steaming sex pot with powerful thrusts.

He jabbed at her time after time with his pulsing powerful cock. His heart pounded in his chest, matching the rhythm of his thrusts.

Across the room, the windowpane reflected their twin images like a mocking voyeur.

Just outside, Jake Putnam threaded his way through the darkness, stepped up to the window that was not covered by a curtain.

Jake had seen the two horses tied by the front porch when he rode up a few minutes before, and although he did not know Bolt's horse by sight, he knew that Bolt was inside. Only two windows of the dark house glowed with light. He had already checked the one at the front of the house. The living room showed no signs of life. He had heard no voices, no noise that would indicate that anyone was home. He had felt his way through the bushes that surrounded the house, rounded the corner and come up at the second window that glowed from the lamp glow.

Moving slowly, he pressed his face up to the window, peeked inside. He saw the naked couple on the bed, recognized Bolt's bare ass bobbing up and down, his dark shaggy hair, the general build. He'd seen Bolt's naked body before, when he climbed out on the balcony at the Sundowners Hotel.

Jake heard the mumbled voices of their love-making then, watched as Bolt jammed into her one last time, then rolled off a minute later, the wet withering cock glistening in the lamp glow.

"Thank you, Bolt," Connie sighed after Bolt had moved off her body. "You're some kind of man."

"And you're some kind of woman," he said. "You're very good." Bolt closed his eyes, fell asleep a few minutes later, contented, fulfilled.

Connie got up, slipped into a long pink sleeping gown, crawled back in bed with Bolt, more satisfied than she had been in a long, long time.

Amylou woke from her deep, thick sleep. She opened her eyes, tried to remember where she was. She thought she had heard voices, people talking, moans and groans, but her mind was still fogged with the medication. Her mouth tasted odd, sour, like she had swallowed a tumbler

115

full of straight alcohol.

A shaft of light fell across the floor of her room. She raised up on her elbow, tried to see into the other room. A dull pain stabbed at her outer thigh, brought her out of the deep fog. That's when she remembered what had happened. She'd been shot! Bolt! Where was he? Was he all right? Had he left her there?

She cocked her head, listened with keen ears. A dog barked somewhere in the distance, but the house was perfectly still.

Panic gripped her as she wondered where Connie was. Maybe the bad men had tracked them there and killed both Bolt and Connie. Maybe the moans and groans she had heard as she came out of her deep sleep came from Bolt, or Connie, as they lay dying in another room.

She eased out of bed, wincing with the pain that pierced her thigh as she moved. She wore only her bright yellow blouse and thin white panties. She limped across the room, following the shaft of light, leaning into the doorway when she got there. She scanned the room next to her bedroom, where the light was coming from. It was the living room and no one was there.

As she hobbled across the living room, she saw another light coming from the hall. Using the wall for support, she made her way down the hall, to the back bedroom, where the other light was shining.

She stopped in the doorframe of the bedroom, stunned by what she saw. Bolt and Connie were in bed together!

Forgetting her wound, she lunged into the room, angered by what she saw, hurt by Bolt's unfaithfulness. She was glad that a sheet covered them. She couldn't bear to see them naked together.

116

Pain stabbed at her wound. She screamed out, stumbled, caught herself before she fell.

Connie woke instantly, jumped out of bed to assist Amylou.

Bolt opened his eyes, sat up in bed, the sheet draped across his lap.

"Amylou, what are you doing in here?" he said, thinking of her wound instead of his own embarrassing situation.

"What are *you* doing in here, you mean!" she lashed out.

Bolt felt his own nakedness beneath the sheet, was glad that Connie had put a nightgown on. Somehow it didn't seem quite so incriminating with her body covered.

"How dare you do this to me, Bolt! You filthy skunk! You rotten, no-good . . ."

"Amylou, please," said Connie gently. "You'll hurt yourself. You shouldn't even be out of bed. Your wound needs time to . . ."

"A lot *you* care," Amylou hissed at Connie. "You get me all doped up, then steal my man right out from under my nose!"

"Amylou!" Bolt said. "I can explain."

"I'll just bet you can! You low-down rat! Well, spare me the details!" she screamed sarcastically. She shook her fists at him, was restrained by Connie, who had her arms around the hysterical girl's waist.

Bolt leaped out of bed, dashed over to help Connie. He grabbed Amylou by the shoulders, shook her, then held her by the chin, forced her to look him in the eyes.

"Shut up and listen to me, Amylou!" he said, his voice harsh, demanding. When he had her attention, his voice

117

became gentle. "I got hit. A piece of a bullet struck my hip. Connie had to dig it out and . . ."

"Oh, Bolt! No! Are you all right?" Her expression changed from anger to one of concern. She looked down at his bare flesh, saw the bandage that covered his wound. "I'm so sorry, Bolt. I just thought . . ."

"Never mind. Connie's right. You shouldn't even be walking on that leg yet."

Tears welled up in her eyes as her emotions caught up with her.

"Bolt, I want to go home."

Bolt scooped her up in his arms, headed for her bedroom.

"Not yet, young lady. You're going back to bed."

As he lowered her into the bed, she looked up at him, the tears about to spill over.

"Bolt, if I die, will you tell Loretta Sweeney so she can handle the business? She's the only one who knows what to do."

"You're not going to die, Amylou. In a few days you'll be up and walking again."

Her mind swam in a sea of darkness as she fought to stay awake.

"Loretta lives in a small house . . . west of town . . . one mile . . . only house there . . . big white fence . . ."

Amylou's head swirled with the black sea as she fell unconscious again.

He walked back to the back bedroom.

"She passed out," he told Connie. "I've got to head out to Eagle Lake and find Bascomb."

Jake Putnam stepped away from the window.

He had to get to Eagle Lake before Bolt did.

He had to warn Bascomb that Bolt was coming.

This was just the thing he'd been waiting for: a chance to prove himself to Bascomb, a chance to become his top man again.

With the information he had, Bascomb would be putty in his hands.

He might even get a healthy bonus.

Chapter Twelve

"You can't ride out now, Bolt," Connie said. "It's a long hard trail and you need your sleep."

"I've got to," Bolt said. "With four men dead, Bascomb's going to find out about it. I want to get to him before he does."

"How's he going to find out about it? Nobody's foolish enough to ride that trail at night."

"I know one who might be."

"Who's that?"

"A man called Jake. I know he rode this far. I was told that he rode on through, but I don't believe it. My hunch is he was still in town when I killed his friends. And if he was in town, then he knows about the four dead men. In fact, I'll bet he's headed to Eagle Lake right now to tell Bascomb the bad news. I've got to leave now, see if I can catch up to him."

"Do you know where Eagle Lake is?"

"South of here."

"And hard to find in the daytime, almost impossible at night unless you know where you're going. If this man Jake is riding there now, then he knows where he's going. You'll never catch him."

"Have you ever been there?" Bolt asked.

"A couple of times when some outlaws drove me down there in a buggy to take care of their men. Gunshot wounds both times. I can tell you how to get there."

"That's good enough for me. Just give me directions."

She explained that he should ride west to the river, follow the river south, about ten miles south of the road that cuts back to Houston.

"That's where it get's tricky," she said. "If you're not watching carefully, you'll ride right on by the cutoff. The country becomes pretty rocky down that way and you've got to look for one special boulder that marks the place where you turn east. The boulder is big, a couple of feet taller than you. It's down by the river, flanked on both sides by cottonwoods. It's got an odd shape. Top heavy, like a mushroom. When you see that boulder, then look off to your left. That would be east. There's an old abandoned miner's shack up on the side of a low hill. That's the point where you head east. The trail goes right by that shack, on up over the hill, then you go until you see the lake. There are several houses and buildings up there, probably more now than when I was there."

"How long ago was that?"

"It's been a couple of years since the last time I was there."

"Sounds easy enough. I think I can find it."

"Bolt, you're not going tonight."

"It'll be daylight by the time I get there."

"Even so, you leave now and it will be slower going in the dark. You can make up what time you might lose by riding in the daytime. Besides, you're going to need all of your senses about you if you're going against Bascomb. You'll be exhausted if you don't get some sleep. One mistake could cost you your life. I'm a nurse, remember. I know how important rest is."

"Yeah, I guess you're right."

"I'll wake you up before dawn. I'll sleep on the couch

121

so I can listen for Amylou. She's going to be mighty sore when she wakes up."

He smiled.

"Yeah. I wouldn't get any sleep at all if you slept with me, would I?"

"No, you wouldn't," she grinned. She slapped him on the butt. "Now get to bed."

Connie didn't need to wake Bolt up. He was up well before dawn. He felt good, well rested. There was no pain in his hip, only tenderness, soreness when he touched it.

He walked into the living room, tried to sneak by Connie without waking her up.

She was a light sleeper and woke up when she felt his presence in the room.

"I'm ready to go," Bolt said.

"Do you want some breakfast first?"

"No. I've got jerky in my saddlebags. I'll be back for Amylou just as soon as I'm through in Eagle Lake." He said it as if he were going to a Sunday picnic, but Connie knew the dangers he faced. She knew that what he was trying to tell her was that he would be back for Amylou, if he lived.

"Don't you worry about her. She really needs to spend the next couple of days in bed. I'll take care of her."

"Thanks, Connie." He looked at her with a special meaning in his eyes. "For everything."

He saw the tears forming in her eyes. She bit her lip, trying to hold them back. She leaned over and kissed him on the cheek.

"Be careful, Bolt."

Bolt recognized the spot where he and Amylou had

122

stopped for lunch the day before, the place where the trail cut back to Houston. So far the trip had been fairly easy, though tiring. He just rode south, keeping the river in sight.

He stopped Nick, let him drink at the river while he munched on some beef jerky, drank from his canteen. He checked his pocket watch, saw that it was almost noon.

He still had a couple of hours to ride, but the longest part of the trip was behind him.

If Jake had ridden to Eagle Lake, then Bolt was still facing five men. His odds hadn't increased one damned bit.

Now all he had to do was follow Connie's instructions, look for the mushroom-shaped rock and the abandoned miner's shack.

Eagle Lake was beyond.

So was trouble.

"Where in the hell have you been all morning?"

Tess had never seen Tom so mad.

"Out shopping," she said.

It was almost noon when she returned to their small room above the Red River Saloon. She held a gift for Tom behind her back.

"Did you take that sock, the one with Bolt's money in it?"

"No. Why would I take that?"

"Well, it's gone!" He lifted the mattress up for the fourth time, ran his hand underneath it. "See, it isn't here."

"You probably moved it and forgot where you put it. Here, I bought this for you."

She brought her hand around in front of her, handed

123

him the fancy new hat.

"Well, I'll be damned," he beamed. "A genuine Stetson! How'd you know I wanted one?"

"I've seen your other hat," she laughed. "It's so battered and dirty. And that bullet hole in it!"

"A badge of courage, my dear," he said, picking up his old hat from the dresser and sticking his finger in the bullet hole, whirling it around on the finger.

He flung the battered hat back on the dresser, stood in front of the mirror and fitted the Stetson to his head, arranging it just so. He adjusted the brim, grinned at himself.

"Now that's class, baby! What's the occasion? It's not my birthday."

"Just 'cause I love you," she cooed, pleased that he liked it. She ran up to him, wrapped her arms around him. She didn't tell him the real reason she had bought the hat. All of his flirting with Loretta Sweeney had not gone unnoticed. He spent a lot of time with that singer, although Loretta didn't seem to return his interest. Tess thought that if she bought Tom a gift, the hat that he really wanted, that he would begin to pay more attention to her. Jealousy, she supposed, although he hated that word.

"Thank you very much," he said as he took her in his arms and kissed her. He looked at himself in the mirror again, grinned. "Now, back to Bolt's sock. I've got to find it. What do you suppose happened to it? You haven't seen it, have you?"

"Not since you stuffed it under the mattress last night, before we went to sleep."

"Beats the hell out of me. Someone must have stolen it. Did you see anyone out in the hall when you left?"

124

"No."

"Anybody pay you a visit while I was gone this morning?"

"Only Loretta."

Tom's heart skipped a beat. Loretta. Of course. She had seen that sock last night when he dropped it out of his pocket in the saloon. When Mr. Harrington had picked it up and joked about it. He remembered now how Loretta had stared at the sock as if she knew its contents. It made sense. Amylou had suspected one of her employees of setting her up for the robbery. Loretta knew how much money Amylou had on hand and when the bills were due. She also knew how much Bolt had won in the poker game. Hell, everybody in town knew about that.

"Did she snoop around while she was here?"

"I doubt it, but I wasn't here all the time."

"You mean you left her alone in this room?"

"Yes, of course. She just came up to change the linens for us, so I talked to her for a while, then left to do the shopping."

"Why would you leave her alone in here?"

"She works here. I don't. I'm sure she locked the door when she left."

"So she changed the sheets. That's it! She stole Bolt's money!"

"Loretta? She wouldn't do that."

"Well, it's gone and she was the only one here. You figure it out." Tom dashed out the door, wearing his new hat.

Tess ran to the door, called down the hall after Tom.

"Where're you going?"

"To see a lady about a sock."

Tom found Loretta downstairs in the small office. He

125

stood in the doorway, his legs spread far apart, his hands clamped to his hips so that his arms formed wings.

"What'd you do with it, Loretta?" he said in an accusing tone.

"Do with what, Tom?" she said, glancing up from the papers on the desk.

"The sock? Where is it?"

She leaned back in her chair and laughed.

"That smelly old thing?"

"It's not smelly," Tom said, "it's . . . never mind. I know you found it. And I know you took it!"

"Yes, I found it and I took it . . . right to the trash can where it belongs. I saw it on the floor when I was making up the bed. It looked so old and faded, I thought you meant to throw it away."

"Did you . . . did you look inside it?"

"Of course not. You said its mate was inside it. Socks don't really thrill me all that much."

"Where's the trash can?"

"Out behind the building, where I put all the trash. The sock'll still be there . . . unless Charlie's already burned the trash."

"Oh, shit, don't tell me things like that!"

Loretta shook her head. She'd seen a lot of things in her life, but never a man so upset about a lousy pair of socks.

"You're some strange man, Tom," she said.

But he didn't hear her. He was already running down the hall to the back door.

He opened the door, ran outside. The trash can was there near the building. It was tipped over on its side, the contents spilled on the ground. Tom breathed a sigh of relief when he saw the blue sock on the ground among the other litter.

A small puppy bounced out from behind the tipped barrel, began yapping at Tom in a fierce, playful voice.

Startled, Tom jumped a foot. His nerves were frayed to the breaking point.

"You dumb dog," Tom said.

The puppy responded to Tom's words by wagging its tail, barking again, then bouncing over to grab Tom's pant leg in its tiny, sharp teeth. The puppy lowered its head with a firm grip on the pant leg and shook his head back and forth. Playful snarls hurled from its mouth as it attacked Tom's pants.

"Get out of here, you mutt," Tom said as he shook his leg, trying to get rid of the small animal. The dog wagged its tail, but didn't let go.

Tom hobbled over to the sock, dragging the puppy with him. He leaned over, reached down to pick up the sock.

Suddenly, the puppy released its hold on Tom's pants, barked once, dashed around Tom's feet and snatched the sock out of Tom's hand.

"No, puppy. Give it to me!"

The puppy held its stance for a moment, looked at Tom and wagged its tail.

Tom reached for the sock. The puppy dashed to the right, stared up at Tom, waiting for its playmate to make the next move, its little tail waving faster.

Tom lunged at the pup. It ran in the other direction, stopped and waited again, its tail still waving in the air. Tom chased him, missed every time he tried to snatch the sock away from the playful puppy.

"Damn it! Give me that sock!"

The puppy ran away from him, the sock dangling from its mouth. Tom gave chase. Just as he caught up with the dog, it changed directions, ran right between Tom's legs.

Tom tripped over the pup, lost his balance. His new Stetson sailed in the air as Tom crashed to the ground. Before he got up, he reached over and retrieved his hat, dusted it off and put it back on his head.

The puppy, tired of waiting for his new friend to chase him, bounced sideways toward Tom.

Tom stayed on the ground, coaxed the puppy to him.

"Come on, puppy. Nice puppy. Give Tom the sock."

The puppy ran over to Tom, stopped right in front of him and dropped the sock, forgetting all about it. He barked at the big creature in front of him, wagged his tail with renewed vigor.

Tom snatched the puppy up in one hand, the precious sock up in the other. He quickly stuffed the sock in his pocket where it would be safe from tiny teeth. He patted the puppy on the head, set it down on the ground.

"Nice, doggy. I'll see that you get some meat scraps."

Tom got up, patted the bulge in his pocket, smiled. He walked back over to the back entrance of the saloon, the puppy trotting after him.

Never again would he lose sight of that damned sock.

Chapter Thirteen

Ernie Gough had been standing at the window most of the morning, except when he was boiling coffee for Bascomb, making biscuits and gravy for the four of them, polishing Bascomb's boots and performing any other menial task the head honcho thought up.

The way the small cabin was situated on a knoll above Eagle Lake, the outlaws could see the trail that led to the lake from the Colorado River—and anyone riding in on that trail.

Bascomb's agitation only added to Ernie's moodiness. Hell, Ord Bascomb was as nervous as a flock of birds before a wind storm. He'd been pacing the floor for the last three hours, stopping every ten minutes at the window to stand next to Ernie, puff on the foul-smelling cigar and peer down at the trail.

Ernie was the newest man in Bascomb's bunch and he had followed Bascomb's orders to a letter, hoping to gain a position of status and authority within the outlaw group. Bascomb had a reputation for heading the roughest, meanest, richest gang in the outlaw world. That's why Ernie Gough had joined him.

But Ernie was disillusioned. He didn't much cotton to the way Bascomb treated him. Ernie never got to participate in the actual robberies; he didn't get his fair share of the take; and the other men, thinking that he was closer to Bascomb than they were, resented him. He could see it in the way they looked at him, the way they tended to ignore him most of the time. But he was nothing but a personal slave to Bascomb.

Even now, Randy Billings and Dan Leacock sat at a table playing poker while Ernie had to stand at the window and watch for Jake Putnam's arrival. The two men used matchsticks instead of money, agreeing to settle up once they got paid for the present job.

Ernie had hired on as a gunnie, not as some lackey to strike matches on. There was no dignity in his job. And even outlaws had dignity.

Ernie stared blankly out the window, not much caring anymore whether Putnam showed up or not. A faint smug smile crossed his lips as he made his decision. After he collected his pay for this job, he was going to split from Bascomb's gang. He'd just take his money and walk away, find himself another outlaw bunch to join. An outlaw bunch with some balls.

"What time is it?" Bascomb asked for the tenth time in the last hour. He stepped up to the window, blew a puff of smoke from his cigar, tapped the ashes to the floor with a finger. He peered out the window, then turned to Ernie.

Ernie Gough dug into his pocket, fished out his gold watch.

"A little past noon."

"I thought he'd be here long before now. Hope nothing went wrong."

Randy Billings turned his head around, looked at his boss with one good eye, one that wouldn't open all the way.

"Don't worry, Ord. No man could face them five and walk away. Not even that Bolt character. Jake probably stopped someplace to get laid." Randy slapped his leg,

130

cackled with that irritating laugh of his.

Bascomb cringed. Randy's harsh laugh was beginning to grate on his nerves. And it was all he could do to look at that ugly face of his with that damned stupid eye that looked like a constant wink, the crooked teeth and busted nose. Maybe, when this job was done, he'd get rid of Billings, just tell him he wasn't needed anymore. He could replace him with Dan Leacock. Dan was quiet, but quick-witted and quick with the draw, probably the best of the lot. He was quiet, without being sullen. He never grumbled about the pay or the condition of the hideout shacks they stayed in, like Billings did. Yes, Dan Leacock would be a good choice. Bascomb felt he could trust him. And that was something he no longer felt about the other men.

Bascomb knew that he was losing control of his boys, and that was making him edgy. Somehow, he had to get it all together again, tighten down on the reins, even if it meant replacing the whole damned bunch.

His reputation was at stake.

"Think that's him coming now," said Ernie Gough.

Bascomb stepped closer to the window, peered out.

"Yeah, that's him. I'd recognize that overgrown horse anywhere. Hope he's got good news."

Billings and Leacock pushed their cards into the middle of the table, gathered up the matchsticks that they would soon need to settle up on the poker game.

Jake rode in slow, tired from the long trip, although he had stopped to sleep on the hard ground when the night riding became too slow and wearing. There was a reason for his slow pace now. He dreaded facing Bascomb, telling him that four of his men had been shot and killed. He especially dreaded telling him that Bolt was the one who

131

had killed them. But Bascomb should be pleased with his other news. At least Jake knew where Bolt was and where he was headed.

Bascomb sat on the edge of the table, waiting for Jake to speak.

Jake stood just inside the room, his hat clasped with both hands in front of him. He tried to find the right words to say what he had to say.

"How'd it go?" Bascomb finally asked.

"They're all dead," Jake blurted out.

Bascomb was stunned by the news that he had lost four of his best men.

"Even Bolt?" Bascomb asked cautiously, a sickening feeling beginning to roll in the pit of his stomach.

"No, not Bolt. Just the four of them. Cripps, Turner, Stoneman and Talley. Bolt's still alive."

"Damn!" mumbled Bascomb as he turned away, tried to collect his thoughts.

"But I know where Bolt is, what his plans are. He's coming to Eagle Lake," Jake said, trying to save face. When Bascomb didn't say anything, Jake babbled nervously, trying to prove to his boss that he had done a good job. "I saw Bolt. And that girlfriend of his, Miss Lovett. They were over to that nurse's house, Miss Gaines, getting patched up. They both got bullet wounds in 'em."

Bascomb still said nothing. His head was turned away from Jake, so Jake couldn't judge his attitude.

"Bolt killed all four of 'em," Jake continued to babble, "One shot apiece. When I found out about it, I tracked him down so's I could find out what he was gonna do. I knew you'd want to know. Miss Lovett was there, her leg all shot up. Bolt was puttin' the boots to that nurse. I

132

stood right outside their window and watched him do it . . ."

Bascomb wheeled around like some angry sea monster rising out of the water. His eyes spewed fire.

"Why in the hell didn't you kill Bolt?" he boomed.

It never occurred to Jake Putnam to kill Bolt. That wasn't his job. Nobody told him to. He was only responsible for reporting to Bascomb once it was over with. And that's what he was doing now. He couldn't understand why Bascomb was so mad.

"I dunno," he said dumbly.

"You stupid asshole!" Bascomb roared, his face bright red with anger. "You had the chance to take him out and you just stand there watchin' him humpin' some hole! Is that how you get your thrills?"

Jake thought Bascomb was going to lunge for his throat. He stood there like a whip-lashed dog, his head lowered, his tail tucked between his legs.

Ernie Gough was still standing by the window, but he was facing the others now. He didn't give a damn whether Bolt was dead or alive. He didn't know the man, didn't care to. He watched Bascomb's temper flare to the point of explosion, was glad that someone else was catching Bascomb's wrath for a change. He'd been the victim of Bascomb's unwarranted temper all too often.

"He probably played with his pud while he was watchin'," cackled Randy Billings, his raucous laughter obscenely irritating. "Didn't you, Jake?"

"Shut up, Randy!" Bascomb screamed, about to explode. He couldn't take any more of Randy's laughter, especially now. Didn't the man have any sensibilities at all?

Randy was secure in his position as Bascomb's right-hand man, second in command. He didn't have to worry that Bascomb had yelled at him just then. The boss was just letting off steam. Randy was used to it, took it in stride.

Dan Leacock leaned back in his chair, quietly observing the interaction between Bascomb and his men. By listening instead of getting involved he was able to see the men more clearly. Bascomb was losing control of his men. The boss was a very insecure man. If he had any backbone of character at all, he would not be reacting as he was. But Bascomb was not strong anymore. He was not even a leader anymore. If he didn't have his men to do his dirty work for him, he would be nothing. And he was losing the men he had because he didn't know how to give them instructions that they could understand. He didn't understand strategy. And the saddest part of all was that Bascomb didn't know he was the way he was.

Bascomb started to lunge at Jake, caught himself in time. He turned and walked across the room, tried to regain his composure. He couldn't let his men see him lose control like that. He had to be strong in this crucial situation. He'd already lost too many men as it was.

Pacing back and forth, he came up with a new plan to get to Bolt. It would work because he knew he was smarter than anyone else.

"I'll tell you what, Jake," he said, strolling back across the room. "I'm going to give you another chance. I want you to ride back into Houston and kill Bolt's side kick, Tom Penrod, I think his name is."

"Penrod? I thought it was Bolt you wanted dusted."

"It is. You see, if we kill his friend, Bolt will run back

to Houston and that's where we'll nail him."

"Why not do it here?" Putnam asked. "He's heading this way."

Bascomb hated it when someone questioned his orders. He felt his temper rising again, quelled it.

"Because Bolt will be more cautious here. He knows what he's facing. Back in Houston, he'll be more concerned about his friend. He won't walk so easy." Bascomb was proud of his plan, his strategy.

"But . . ." Jake started to say.

"You want the job or not?" Bascomb snapped. "There's a hundred-dollar bonus in it if you do the job right."

Jake beamed at the chance to redeem himself, gloated over the fact that he'd get a bonus.

"Yes, I'll do it."

"Good. Just see Sheriff Connors when you first get to Houston. He'll arrange everything for you."

"Don't worry, Bascomb, I can handle it."

Bascomb turned to the man at the window.

"Ernie, fix us some lunch. We'll all eat, then Jake can be on his way."

Ernie did as he was told, hoping it would be the last tme he would have to take an order from the man. As soon as he got his money, he was going to go his own way.

After Putnam left for Houston, Ernie cleared the dishes from the table, prepared to wash them. The other three men remained at the table, Billings and Leacock sitting across from Bascomb. With food in his belly and his new plan to get Bolt being carried out, Bascomb felt better, more confident of himself. There was only one more detail he had to handle: how to get Bolt back to Houston.

Drawing a fresh cigar out of his pocket, Bascomb pondered the situation. He sure as hell didn't want to be around when Bolt showed. If Bolt could outsmart four of his best men, chances were he could do the same thing here in Eagle Lake. No, he'd wait and catch Bolt off guard in Houston. He'd have to leave a man here to confront Bolt, a man who could convince Bolt to go back to Houston. But which one could do the job without getting killed himself? From what he'd heard of Bolt, the man wouldn't draw his pistol unless someone drew on him first, so that would be no problem. He glanced around the room at the other three men, made his decision.

Things were coming to a head, Bascomb knew, and he could already see how they were going to turn out. In fact, he might get more out of the deal than he had planned if everything went as smooth as he figured.

"This might be the chance we're looking for," he told the men across from him. "Connors has been wanting that saloon of Miss Lovett's for a long time—the Red River Saloon. If my little scheme works out, we're going to get a piece of the action, and believe me, that saloon is a sweet little money maker. If the robbery didn't bust her, then what we're doing is going to help things along. By killing Bolt and his friend, Miss Lovett will be too scared to stay there. She already knows she has no protection from the sheriff. Connors made that pretty clear to her. Connors will be able to pick that saloon up for a song, and since we're the ones who are forcing her out of business, he'll have to share the profits with us."

Neither of the men said anything.

"Leacock, I'm going to leave you here in Eagle Lake to

136

face Bolt alone. Tell him that his friend is dead. That'll force him to return to Houston. Don't worry, he won't kill you unless you draw on him first."

"What if he shoots first and asks questions later?" Dan asked calmly, just to see Bascomb's reaction.

"You answer his questions first, Dan. Think you can do it?"

"No problem."

Bascomb admired Dan's courage. Most men would be frightened out of their wits to face Bolt alone, but Dan was very calm about it. He knew that he had made the right decision to let Billings go and move Dan Leacock up into the top place as his right-hand man. He would make the change just as soon as Bolt was dead.

"And where are we going to be while all this is going on between Dan and Bolt?" Randy Billings asked.

"We're going to ride on out to that hideout cabin near Houston, hole up there until it's time to go after Bolt."

"You ain't scared of that bastard, are you, boss?" Billings laughed, the sound of his cackling voice sending chills straight to Bascomb's brain.

Bascomb controlled his rising temper, glad that Dan Leacock would soon be his top man.

Leacock was pleased with the new assignment. He had no fear of this man named Bolt. From what he had learned about Bolt, he knew that the man had more character than Bascomb. Bolt would not draw on him because Dan had no reason to pull his pistol on the stranger.

Dan would deliver Bascomb's message to the stranger called Bolt. Then he would ride south, find a new life for himself.

137

*　　　*　　　*

Bolt cursed out loud.

He knew he had missed the trail to Eagle Lake.

The countryside was changing again. It was no longer rocky. In fact he hadn't seen anything that looked like a boulder in over an hour. He pulled his pocket watch out, checked the time. According to his calculations, he should be riding into Eagle Lake right about now, and he hadn't even found the trail that led to it.

He turned Nick around, headed back north.

An hour later, he spotted the boulder that Connie had told him about. It was the only good-sized rock on the entire trip. He had seen it before, but hadn't recognized it from her description. If that boulder looked like a mushroom, he'd eat his hat. It was flat on the top, went straight down on one side. The only part that even resembled a mushroom was the left side of it where it jutted out, curved down to the thick base.

Another reason why he had missed the boulder was because when he had stopped there briefly before, he had looked for the other landmark she had mentioned: the old abandoned miner's shack up in the foothills, off to the left. The foothills were there, but no shack.

Bolt decided this had to be the place, although there wasn't much of a trail. He turned east, rode up to the foothills.

He saw it then. The traces of the shack. Burned to the ground. Only pieces of charred wood remained to mark the trail. He stopped there, glanced back down to the river.

Maybe Connie hadn't been so far off at that.

From this angle, the boulder looked very much like an overgrown mushroom.

Bolt checked his pistol, shoved it back in its holster.

It had been a slow, tiring ride, and yet he knew the roughest part was still ahead of him.

Somewhere back up in those hills, near a peaceful lake, were five men.

They waited for him.

So did death.

Chapter Fourteen

Sheriff Connors didn't bother to get up when Jake Putnam walked into his office. He looked around Jake, expecting Bascomb to be with him. He didn't like waiting this long for his share of the robbery money.

"Where's Bascomb?" he asked.

"He's riding in from Eagle Lake. Him and the boys'll hole up at the shack. He sent me in to take care of Bolt's sidekick. Said you'd set it up."

"What about Bolt? Is he . . . dead?" Connors leaned forward, spoke in a low voice, even though there was no one else in the room.

"Bascomb's pretty pissed about that. You were supposed to keep him here in town."

Connors reached up and felt the lump on the top of his head, winced at the pain.

"I know. We had a slight altercation. I hear the girl rode out with him. Amylou Lovett."

When the sheriff didn't offer him a chair, Jake grabbed one that was against the wall, pulled it across the floor and plunked it down in front of Connor's desk. The scraping sound sent a shiver across the fine hairs on the back of Connors' neck. He sat down, the weight of his tall, firm body causing the spindly chair legs to wobble. He slouched down in the chair, his long legs stretched out in front of him.

"Yair. They both got tore up pretty bad by bullets, but

they're still alive." Jake made it sound much worse than it was.

"Where'd they take the bullets?" Connors asked, picturing Bolt and Amylou with bloody chest wounds, perhaps Bolt's face blown away.

"Amylou's leg was almost blown away. If she lives, she won't be up and walking for a long spell. But you know how those things can go. Gangrene, loss of blood, infection. No tellin' if she'll make it or not."

"What about Bolt?" Damn, he wished Putnam would tell it straight, get to the point. It was like pulling teeth to get any information out of him. But Connors tried to be patient. He knew he had a good thing going with Bascomb and his bunch. He was already getting rich from the kickbacks on the last three jobs. Bascomb and his boys did all the dirty work and all Connors had to do was look the other way, pretend he didn't see anything. And for that, Bascomb paid him twenty-five percent of the take. Not bad, but he was getting greedy. From now on he was going to ask for a bigger cut of the pie. Fifty-fifty. Straight down the middle.

"Funny thing about Bolt. None of the witnesses could agree about whether he took a bullet or not. Some swore he did, some said not. But he got hit. I was the only one who saw him afterwards. I ought to know."

"Damn it, where'd he get hit?"

"In the hip. He . . ."

"Can he walk? Can he ride?"

"Yep."

Connors leaned back in his chair, ran his hand over his chin. With a sickening feeling, he realized that if Bolt was gun shot, still alive, then chances were, he'd taken out one of the boys.

141

"Who bought it?"

Feeling important that he knew more than the sheriff, Jake sat up in his chair, leaned forward and spoke in a low, confidential voice.

"Four of 'em. Cripps, Turner, Stoneman and Talley." Jake rattled off their names for the second time that day. "Probably Dan Leacock, too, by now."

Connors reeled back, stunned by the news.

"Jeeezus!" Connors pushed his chair back, leaned down and opened the bottom drawer of his desk. He pulled out two tumblers, a bottle of whiskey. "Want a drink?"

"No thanks, Sheriff. I never drink when I'm working. And I still got a job to do." His remark was sarcastic, but it went over Connors' head. Jake had heard Bascomb grumble about how much booze the sheriff drank. Jake wondered if Connors had been drinking the morning he was supposed to keep Bolt from chasing after them. More than likely he was.

Pouring himself a healthy drink, Connors downed it in one gulp, put the bottle and glasses back in the drawer.

Connors leaned back in his chair again, let the whiskey warm his belly.

"So Bascomb sent you to take Penrod out of the picture. Yes, I can make the arrangements." He stood up, swelled out his massive chest, walked across the floor while he thought about it. He walked back over, faced Jake. "You know that small saloon down the street, around the corner? Big Hank's, where all the outlaws go?"

"Yair, I been in there."

"You go down there and wait so you won't be conspicuous or noticed. I'll send one of my deputies to fetch

142

you when the time is right."

"Where's Penrod?" Jake asked.

"He's stayin' at the Red River Saloon, in one of the rooms upstairs. Him and his girlfriend, Tess Hummer. But you can't just walk in there and blast them away. I know who can help us, though."

"Who's that?"

Connors ignored his question.

"You wait at Big Hank's until my deputy comes for you. We'll have to wait until Penrod takes his woman to bed. Then you go into the saloon and call Tess downstairs. Tom will come down after her. You can shoot him on the stairs, slip on out the back door before anyone knows you were there."

"Sounds like it might work. But it's risky. If it doesn't work the way you think . . ."

"It will, Putnam. You'll be backed up by someone there in the saloon."

"Who?"

"Never mind that. You just worry about your end of it."

Connors stood up, walked to the door of his office. He called Deputy Thorp into the room.

"Will I have time to grab a bite to eat first?" Jake asked before the deputy got there.

"Yes. It'll take me a half hour to make the arrangements. Then it'll depend on how horny Penrod is, when he decides to take Tess upstairs to screw her to the bed."

Deputy Thorp was a young man. Neat, clean-cut, freshly shaved.

"Come in, Thorp," Connors said. "This here's Jake. He's going to go down to Big Hank's to wet his whistle. I'll need you to deliver a message to him later. Just wanted

143

you to meet him so's you'd recognize him."

The men did not shake hands, just nodded at each other.

"Good luck, Jake," Connors said, dismissing him.

When Jake was gone, Connors turned to Thorp.

"I need to run an errand. You stay here and watch the shop. Then, when I get back, I need you to do something for me. Now listen carefully. You know that new feller in town, Tom Penrod?"

"Yeah. I've seen him around. It was his friend that got robbed out of his poker money, wasn't it?"

"Yeah, I think it was. Anyways, I want you to go over to the Red River Saloon when I get back, have yourself a drink or two. I'm buying. Just keep your eye on Penrod and his girlfriend, Tess Hummer. I want to know when he takes her up to bed. When you see them go upstairs, give 'em about fifteen minutes to get settled in, then go on down to Big Hank's. Just tell Jake that it's time."

"Time for what? Is that all you want me to tell him?"

"Yes. He'll understand."

Deputy Thorp scratched his head, puzzled.

"But why would you want to know when Penrod takes his lady friend to bed? Seems like kind of a personal thing to me."

"We're just going to play a little practical joke on Penrod," Connors said, a cruel smile on his face. "Just a harmless little prank."

Bolt didn't like the lay of the land. The hills and bluffs, gulches, valleys and outcroppings of huge rocks.

Too many places for a man to lay waiting to ambush him.

His eyes constantly darted about, searching the cracks

144

and crevices he passed, looking ahead to the bluffs, checking his backtrail. He rode with the reins in his left hand, his shooting hand near the butt of his holstered pistol.

It was quiet out here on the desolate trail. Too damned quiet. He knew there would be someone waiting for him when he arrived at Eagle Lake. He just didn't know where they'd be waiting.

Something caught his eye. Something shiny like the metal of a rifle barrel glistening in the afternoon sun.

He tensed in the saddle. His hand slid over to touch the butt of his pistol. He looked in the direction where he'd glimpsed the reflection.

He saw it again. Knew what it was. The lake, off to his left, reflecting the sun that was about to drop beyond the horizon. He eased his muscles, moved his hand away from the pistol.

He stopped up ahead, where he had a clear view of the lake and the buildings surrounding it. Not too many buildings there. Maybe a dozen or so. A couple of horsemen riding together. He wondered if they were part of Bascomb's bunch.

He touched his boots to Nick's side, rode on, moving out slow and cautious.

His eyes focused on the small community below him, he almost missed the movement to his right. He tensed again. His heart skipped a beat. His hand was a blur as it shot to his Colt .45. When he looked, he saw the horse that had caught his attention with its movement. The horse was tied to a tree, just beyond a huge rock formation by the side of the trail.

The thin hairs on the back of his neck bristled as if blown by a gentle summer breeze. Cords of tension

145

rippled through his arm and shoulder muscles.

His hand hovered above the holster, but he did not draw.

He drew the reins back, stopping Nick in his tracks. Moving slow and quiet, he slid his leg across the saddle, let himself down to the ground.

His saddle squeaked at the shifting weight. Bolt cursed, held fast. He figured whoever was up there hiding behind the rock hadn't seen him coming. Otherwise Bolt would have made a perfect target as he rode up the trail. His only chance now was to sneak up on the man, catch him while he wasn't looking.

He dashed across the road, moving on tip toes. He reached the face of the towering rock, he stopped, listened with keen ears.

The tree-tied horse snorted.

Bolt's heart pounded in his chest. He listened. Heard no other sound.

Another boulder, almost as tall as the one he was standing in front of now, rested on the ground some ten feet beyond. If he could reach it without getting shot, then he could go around back of that rock, come up behind it and get a look at whoever was back there.

He judged the distance again, decided he could make it.

He rested the palm of his hand on the butt of his pistol, ready to draw in a hurry. He took a deep breath, ducked his head down, and ran like hell.

He made it half way across.

Dan Leacock stepped out from behind the first rock, his hand poised above his holstered pistol.

Bolt stopped dead in his tracks, caught out in the open. As he whirled around to face the man, his fingers slid around the pistol butt.

146

He paused, waited for the man to draw on him. He watched the man's hand.

The two men faced each other, each waiting for the other to make the first move. The slightest move from either of them would set off the fatal explosions.

They stared at each other, neither of them moving.

"You looking for me?" Leacock asked evenly.

"Your name Bascomb?"

"No."

"You work for him?"

"I did."

The men were still rigid in their stances. Both were ready to shoot at the drop of a hat. They were testing each other, waiting like mountain lions, ready to pounce on their prey.

"Where's Bascomb?" Bolt asked, his voice calm and even.

"I can't say," said Leacock with equal calmness.

"Or you won't say." There was a hard steel cast to Bolt's gaze.

"You read me right."

"What's your name?"

"The name's Leacock, Bolt."

So the man knew his name. Something funny was going on. Bolt wanted to look around, check to see if Bascomb or someone else was waiting behind the other boulder. But he didn't dare turn his head. If he glanced away for even an instant, Leacock could blow him away.

"Bascomb send you here to kill me?"

"He sent me here. To give you a message." Leacock relaxed his stance, let his hand fall away from his pistol butt, his arm hanging straight down at his side.

"What's the message?" Bolt kept his hand on his

weapon, suspecting a trick. Leacock was too calm, too sure of himself. A man didn't act that way unless he had someone to back him up.

Without moving his head away, Bolt's eyes darted to the right, then to the left. He saw no shadows lurking behind either rock formation, no movement, no sound besides the beating of his own heart.

"Your friend, Tom Penrod, is dead by now. Assassinated."

"No, I don't believe you!" Bolt was stunned. He couldn't imagine Tom dead. He dropped both hands to his sides, shaken by the possibility the man was telling the truth. "How do you know?" he said finally, a slight tremble to his voice.

"Bascomb sent one of his men to kill your friend."

"That doesn't mean he succeeded."

"No. But there was no chance of failure. There were men in Houston to back him up."

"What men?"

"I've delivered my message, Bolt. That's all I have to say."

"One of Amylou's employees? The sheriff?" Bolt asked, pressing the issue.

Leacock did not answer. Bolt thought about drawing on him, forcing him to tell him what he wanted to know at gunpoint. It wouldn't work, he knew. A man like Leacock wouldn't talk unless he wanted to.

"How long ago did he leave? This man who was sent to kill Penrod?"

"About three hours ago."

Bolt swore a silent oath. If he hadn't missed the cutoff to the lake the first time around, he would have had a slim chance of making it back to Houston in time. But as it was, someone could be killing Tom at this very minute.

Bolt had never felt so helpless in his life. He wanted to lash out at something. He wanted to kill Leacock for telling him.

"Is Bascomb still in Eagle Lake?"

"No," Leacock answered. He saw the pain in Bolt's eyes, the compassion for another human being. That was something he had never seen in Bascomb. He wanted to tell Bolt all he knew, but he wouldn't. He didn't want revenge. He just wanted to walk away.

"Did he go to Houston?"

"He headed that way."

"Well, the next time you see that bastard, tell him I'll shoot him on sight. I won't even give him a chance to draw."

"I won't be seeing him again. I'm riding south."

Bolt turned and walked away, knowing that Leacock would not shoot him. He mounted Nick, headed toward Houston. He was in a hell of a hurry.

Bolt knew he was too late to warn Tom.

By the time he got to Houston, Tom's fate would already be decided.

Chapter Fifteen

"Good evening, Virgil. Haven't seen you for a few days," Loretta Sweeney smiled.

"Evenin', ma'am. The sheriff keeps me pretty busy these days," said Deputy Sheriff Virgil Thorp. "Howdy, Mr. Harrington. Tell the Missus she cooked up a mighty fine supper tonight."

"The Missus? What are you talking about? I cooked that food myself." Red Harrington loved to kid with the younger generation. It made him feel younger himself. "Come on, pull up a chair. I'm just about to leave."

"Don't leave on my account," Thorp said as he scooted a chair back and sat down at the table.

"My Kathleen'll be waitin' for me. Next time you're in the cafe, stop by the kitchen and watch me cook." He smiled, finished his drink and set the glass on the table. "Good night, Loretta. Enjoyed your singing, as usual. See you tomorrow."

"Thanks, Pops."

As the older man was leaving, Thorp glanced at the couple at the next table. Tom Penrod and Tess Hummer sat across from each other, talking and laughing. Thorp had spotted them when he walked in, was glad that he found a table so close. He could keep his eye on them, know when they were ready to retire for the night. Thorp didn't know what kind of a practical joke the sheriff and his friend were cooking up for Penrod, but the tall, lanky man seemed to have a sense of humor. Maybe he wouldn't mind.

"Did they find the men who robbed you yet?" Thorp asked Loretta.

"I don't know. We haven't heard a word from Bolt or Amylou. I'm really worried about them," Loretta said, her brow wrinkled with a frown.

"Don't think you have to worry, Loretta. If the robbers had wanted to kill them, they had the opportunity when they took the money. From what I've heard about that Bascomb bunch, they can disappear into thin air after they make a hit. Your friends are probably still tracking them."

"I hope you're right." Loretta wanted to believe the young deputy, but something caught in her throat when she thought about it, like she was afraid to breathe. Her stomach quivered with queasiness. It was as if she couldn't force herself to concentrate on what might be happening to Amylou, her closest friend, and yet she could think of nothing else. She wanted to free herself from the feeling that something was about to happen.

"I thought Sheriff Connors would send me out with a posse to investigate this case, but he said Bolt wanted to handle it himself."

"You know how the sheriff feels about Amylou running this saloon, being a woman and all that. You want a drink? I'll call Carl over."

"I never drink when I'm working."

"You working now?"

"Not exactly, but the sheriff is going to be busy tonight and he asked me to watch the jail till he gets back."

"Well, I hope you'll stick around. It's time for me to sing another song."

151

"I'm sure I'll be here a while," he said, glancing at the couple at the next table.

Thorp didn't have to wait as long as he thought he would. Shortly after Loretta started to sing, Tess whispered something in Penrod's ear, took his hand and led him toward the staircase.

After waiting the prescribed fifteen minutes to allow Tom and his girl to get settled in their room, Deputy Virgil Thorp rose from his chair, walked out of the Red River Saloon unnoticed.

Thorp headed for Big Hank's where he would find the man named Jake.

It was time for Jake to play a practical joke.

Tom was more worried about Bolt than he let on.

He didn't like the odds Bolt was facing, hadn't liked them from the beginning. He had wanted to accompany his friend to track the robbers, to be there if Bolt ran into trouble, but Bolt had insisted that Tom stay here and keep an eye on the employees. Bolt was stubborn that way, sometimes, and Tom knew better than to buck him.

Tom had been watching the three employees pretty carefully since Bolt had given chase, but so far, he hadn't detected any suspicious activities by any of them.

Loretta Sweeney was the mysterious one because she never talked about herself, her past life, but that made her even more intriguing, as far as Tom was concerned.

Tom didn't really care for the other two employees, but that didn't mean they were guilty of anything. The bartender, Carl Anders, was the one Tom watched the most. There was something about that man that rubbed Tom the wrong way. Carl was tight-lipped and shifty-eyed, about as friendly as a coiled snake. He was also quick to anger when things didn't go his way.

When Tom had observed Cole Megan, he saw that the dealer had lightning-fast hands, a quick draw with the pistol when trouble developed over a poker game. But since the robbery, he had been friendly enough. Almost too friendly.

Tom was glad Tess wanted to retire early that night. He had spent enough time sitting in the saloon during the past two days that it was beginning to make him edgy. He found it increasingly difficult to hang around the saloon and talk to the customers, exchanging idle conversation, when he was so worried about Bolt.

He knew it was getting to Tess, too. She was a quiet, loving girl and she didn't like to spend her time in a saloon. Tom sensed her jealousy, especially where Loretta was concerned. He knew that was why she had bought him the new Stetson, so that he would pay more attention to her. But she had nothing to be jealous about. Not that he wouldn't have taken Loretta to bed if he could have, but Loretta hadn't responded to his advances.

It was good to be with Tess tonight. She had a way of calming his shattered nerves. He needed her touch tonight. He felt very mortal, as if his whole world was going to explode around him. They undressed quickly, climbed into bed together without having to talk about it.

He took her savagely, pounding his thick, rigid cock into her like a lust-crazed animal, not much caring whether she liked it or not. Tonight he had to have her that way.

He pressed his lips hard against hers when he kissed

153

her, mashing them against her teeth. He crushed her breasts in his hands, squeezed her nipples as if to pulverize them into chicken feed. He slammed against her thighs, pounding her flesh with his strength. He drove into her sex folds with his powerful, throbbing shaft, lashing out with his anger, his frustrations, his need to strike out, to hurt.

When he climaxed, he spilled more than his seed. For that one brief moment of timelessness, he was released from his rage, his feeling of helplessness. He was suddenly drained of the fear that had eaten him away.

"Listen, Tom," she said a few minutes later, turning her head, straining her ear. "Someone's calling me."

Snatching her dress from the chair, she held it in front of her, opened the door.

"Tess! Tess! Come downstairs. Quick!" It was Loretta's voice.

"What do you want?" Tess called back.

"Your old friend is here, asking for you," came the voice from below.

"Who is it?" Tess called.

"Says his name is Putnam," Loretta answered. "Hurry!"

Tess backed into the room, slipped her dress on, stepped into her shoes.

"Who's Putnam?" asked Tom, startled by the commotion.

"I don't know him, but he rides with Bascomb. Maybe he knows something about Amylou." She dashed out the door, buttoning her dress as she ran down the stairs.

She was gone before Tom realized that something was wrong. It struck him like a bolt of lightning. He shook his head, tried to figure out what was happening. Still naked, he opened the door a crack, listened with careful ears.

It was very quiet downstairs. The talk and laughter had died out. He didn't like it.

He closed the door, dressed quickly. He checked his pistol, slid it into the holster. He opened the door again, listened. There were no screams, no sounds of a struggle downstairs.

Only an eerie stillness that he didn't know whether it came from downstairs, or inside himself, where the sound of his pounding heart blotted out everything else.

He snatched his hat from the table, jammed it onto his head. Stepped out of the room, which was at the far end of the hallway.

He checked to his right, peered into the empty blackness of the window at his end of the hall. There were no dark shadows hovering on the balcony beyond the faceless window pane.

He glanced to his left, looked down the length of the hall, watching for someone to move around the corner of the hall, where the staircase joined the two floors of the saloon.

He heard the whisper of a boot scuffle across the floor, didn't know if it was on the stairs or echoed from below. Noises sounded different when everything was so still.

He froze, his breath stopped in midair. He listened, his ears keen. The silence deafened him.

A man coughed downstairs. The noise fluttered up the stairs, jangled across Tom's nerves like a bow's sudden twang when released of its arrow.

He listened again, his ears pounding with the silence. There was no clatter of cards. No click of the chips, nor

155

rattle of dice. No clink of glass. No voices. It was as if the people in the saloon had suddenly been swallowed by a giant vacuous balloon and carried off to another world.

"Tess!" he called. "Tess, are you all right?"

He heard only a muffled reply that was quickly choked off.

He listened again. The silence was even more crushing than before.

Tom took a cautious step, easing his foot to the floor. A board creaked with his shifting weight. The sound of it multiplied, pierced Tom's ears.

He paused. Listened. Waited.

Hugging the wall, he snuck down the hall, one careful step after the other. Step. Pause. Listen. Step . . . pause . . . listen.

The stairway was just beyond the corner wall, tucked away so that he could not see if anyone was on the steps.

He eased his hat off his head, grasped it firmly between his thumb and forefinger. His other hand rested on the butt of his pistol.

Holding the Stetson head-high, he edged it toward the corner of the walls.

The stillness exploded with fireworks. A bullet caught the Stetson, sent it whirling in the air. More shots rang out. Before the hat hit the floor, it bounced like a puppet, taking each bullet and spitting it out.

Tom backed away, turned quickly, ran for the window at the other end of the hall.

Footsteps pounded on the stairs.

Tom didn't take time to look back.

He crashed through the window in a headlong dive. Shards of jagged glass showered over Tom as he slammed into the railing of the outside balcony. Stunned, he couldn't move for an instant.

Footsteps pounded down the hall, approaching the balcony beyond the smashed window. Closer and closer.

Tom recovered from the shock of slamming into the railing. His eyes darted up to the window. He saw Jake Putnam racing toward him, his scarred face outlined by the jagged glass around the window frame. Jake's pistol was cocked and aimed, the long black hole of the barrel trained on Tom's head.

Instantly, Tom rolled away, drew his pistol. It was cocked and aimed as it cleared leather. He squeezed the trigger before Putnam could focus his eyes on the darkness of the balcony outside the window.

Putnam's shoulder exploded in a blossom of blood, small crimson droplets spraying out in the air, splattering against the jagged edges of the broken window, staining his shirt.

Putnam's body jerked back from the impact of the speeding bullet. His scream echoed the gunshot, rippling through the night like a thundering wave at floodtide. His pistol clattered to the floor as he released his grip, grasped at the pain in his shoulder. Struggling to retain his balance, he staggered forward, bounced against the window ledge, then plummeted headlong through the broken window.

Tom's response was instant.

He grabbed Putnam by the collar, jerked him closer. He slammed his knee across the wounded man's throat, exerted pressure as he held his pistol to Putnam's temple.

The light from the hall spilled out onto the balcony now that Putnam was no longer blocking the window.

Tom looked at the man's face.

"You're Jake, you scar-faced bastard! Where's Bolt?"

"I—I don't know."

"Yes you do!" Tom pushed his knee harder into Putnam's throat.

"He's at . . . Eagle . . . Lake," Putnam choked, barely able to draw in a breath.

"Is the sheriff in on this?" Tom demanded.

Jake didn't answer.

Tom thrust his knee against Jake's vocal cord, rammed the pistol barrel against his head.

"Yes!"

Tom eased up with his leg.

Putnam gasped and sputtered, fought for breath.

"Who else?" Tom asked.

Out of the corner of his eye, Tom saw a shadow appear at the broken window, once again blocking off the light.

"Who's backing you up?" he demanded quickly, shoving against Jake's throat.

Jake opened his mouth to answer.

A flame erupted in the darkness, a split second before the shot rang out. It came from the window.

Putnam's head exploded, his face torn away by the blast. Blood and gray brain matter sprayed across the balcony, the railing, the wooden walkway. Jake was dead instantly.

Tom whirled around, shot at the empty window just as the shooter ducked down.

Tom shot again, scrambled over the railing, dropped down with a thud to the ground below.

He escaped into the night, the shots still ringing out in the night. While the people in the saloon began running up the stairs to see who had been shot, Tom ran around

158

front, untied his horse from the hitchrail, and rode off before anyone knew he was gone.

A half hour later, the night skies opened up, releasing the cleansing rain that had been building all day.

Tom tipped his head back, allowing the gentle rain to wash away some of the horror that was emblazoned in his brain.

Chapter Sixteen

The brilliant bolt of lightning etched a silver, jagged slash across the black sheet of night. Four seconds later its rumbling thunder cracked the air as if it had stopped to take a breath before emitting its booming belch.

Bolt cursed, stuck the palm of his hand out in the darkness to test for moisture. The gentle rain was just beginning. He didn't mind getting soaked to the skin, but he sure as hell hated being out in the open during a thunder storm.

He had no idea how far he was from Houston, but he had seen no signs of civilization since darkness covered the land. No homey lanterns glowing from house windows. No burning fires that usually dotted the landscape of darkness. He hadn't even smelled the smoke from wood-burning cook stoves.

It was hard, riding at night like that, when the sky had been so black and he couldn't be sure he was still on the trail that led to Houston. He had been able to keep riding by varying his pace, riding fast for a while, then slowing to let his horse catch its breath. But in the darkness, he felt no sense of speed or progress. At times it seemed as if his horse were running in place, getting nowhere in a hurry.

Lightning streaked the sky again. Bolt counted the seconds until the thunder cracked. He judged the lightning to be about four miles away.

His stomach knotted up every time he thought about Tom. He knew that Tom was a good shot, but if they caught him off guard, anything could happen. It was too late to think about that. From what Leacock told him, Tom would have already faced the problem. He was either dead or alive. It was as simple as that. And yet it was the not knowing that ate at Bolt. He just couldn't imagine life without Tom around to keep him laughing. It wasn't just the kidding they did with each other. It was the good times they shared, the sad times, the dangerous ones.

The lightning came oftener now as the rain increased. Bolt was drenched, but he didn't seem to notice. He wondered if he was riding around in a big circle, with no beginning and no end, no place to jump off.

He saw it when the lightning flashed again. The first glimmer of hope. Off in the distance, when the earth was bathed in its brief illumination, Bolt had seen something shiny. Not a glimmer from a lantern or a fire, but a brief sparkle from a reflection. Like water on a tin roof or a small pond.

He snapped the reins, patted Nick on the shoulder, urging the horse to a faster pace.

Ten minutes later, he knew what was catching the lightning's glow and reflecting it like a lighthouse in a storm.

A white fence, surrounding a house and a yard. It was the only house around and he knew it belonged to Loretta Sweeney. Amylou had described it perfectly. He didn't see the glow from the curtained window until he was near the yard. Loretta was home.

From where he sat on his horse near the fence, he was able to see the first lights of the city of Houston. A mile away, according to Amylou.

161

His first instinct was to ride on into Houston, but he couldn't wait, even another mile, to learn about Tom. Loretta was sure to know.

He rode through the open gate, spotted a barn when the storm gave its light. He rode on in, heard another horse nicker in the darkness. He drew a match out of his pocket, tried to light it. The match was soggy, useless. When the lightning flashed again, he was able to spot a lantern, dry matches.

He lit the lamp, set it down and tied Nick to the rail of one of the stalls.

"Wait for me, boy," he said, patting Nick on the rump. "I'll be right back."

He carried the lantern with him, headed for the house. His boots sloshed in the puddles, slipped in the mud.

"Hello, the house!" he called out as he stepped up on the porch. "Loretta, it's Bolt!" He couldn't wait any longer to find out about Tom. He pounded on the door, desperate to talk to the woman inside.

A minute later, Loretta unlatched the bolts, opened her door. When she saw Bolt, she gasped, stepped back to allow him to enter. She was already dressed for bed.

"Bolt! You're alive! Thank God!" She threw her arms around his drenched body, hugged him tight, smiled.

Bolt was surprised by her show of concern. He still suspected that she might be the one who set up the robbery, but he didn't care right then. He just wanted to know about Tom.

"Where's Amylou?" she asked before Bolt could ask about Tom. "Is she . . . is she . . ."

"She's fine," Bolt assured her. "A bullet wound in her leg, but she'll be good as new. What about T . . ."

"You're soaked. Come in and get out of those wet

162

clothes." Loretta grabbed Bolt's arm, pulled him inside and closed the door.

"Loretta, what about Tom?" he said quickly. He drew in a breath, waited for her response.

Her face saddened.

Bolt's heart sank.

"Someone tried to kill him. Isn't that terrible?"

"Tried?" Bolt was afraid to let his breath out. His shoulders tensed. His eyes searched hers for an answer.

"Yes. But the man was killed instead. Tom escaped."

Bolt's shoulders slumped as the tension flooded out of him. He expelled the trapped air, took a deep breath.

"Who tried to . . ." Bolt started to say.

"Is Tess . . ." Loretta said at the same time.

They both laughed, an hysterical laugh that came from extreme tension, from the release of pent-up emotions.

"I reckon we better either take turns or draw straws to see who goes first." Bolt looked at Loretta, saw her for the first time. The lines of her face no longer seemed hard or harsh. There was a gentleness in her eyes, an understanding that was not there before.

"Yes, I guess we both have a lot of questions. Jake Putnam was the man who tried to kill Tom. I guess he's one of Bascomb's men. But, he's dead now."

"Did Tom kill him?"

"There's some question about that. But, I don't see how Tom could have done it since Putnam was shot in the head at close range. Putnam had a shoulder wound too, and everybody seems to think that's where Tom shot him. Evidently, Tom jumped through the balcony window at the end of the hall when Jake went after him. Then, when Tom shot him, he fell through the same window, ended up on the balcony with Tom."

"Tell me every detail you can remember about it. Maybe I can figure it out."

"Well, I saw this Putnam fellow come into the saloon. I didn't know him from Adam. He didn't order a drink or anything. He just walked through the room, then walked over to the stairway, leaned against the wall. I thought he was waiting for one of the glitter gals. Cole Megan told me to call Tess downstairs. She and Tom had already gone up to bed. Anyway, Megan said Putnam was a friend of Tess', so I called her down."

"Did she come down?"

"Yes and the next thing I knew, shots were being fired upstairs. There were several shots and when it was all over, people started running up the stairs to see what happened."

"Did the bartender, Carl Anders, go upstairs after the shooting?"

"No."

"Who did?"

"All of them, eventually."

"What about Tess? Did she know what was going on?"

"No. Megan held his hand over her mouth when Tom came looking for her. Tom called out to her but Megan wouldn't let her answer."

"Hmmm. Was Megan upstairs when the last shot was fired?"

"He may have been. It was all so confusing."

"Where's Tom now?"

"No one's seen him since the shooting. He's probably hiding out someplace. But we can find him in the morning."

"I've got to talk to him."

"Well, you can't go into town tonight. Bascomb's

probably got some of his men in there looking for you. You can stay here."

"You're probably right about Bascomb," he said, thinking what Leacock had told him about Bascomb heading for Houston.

"Now get out of those wet clothes or you'll catch cold. I'll hang them up to dry."

Bolt looked down, saw the puddle by his feet. "Sorry about your floor."

"Never mind that. Will Amylou be all right?"

"Sure. A nurse in Etinger is taking care of her, keeping her in bed for a couple of days. I'll go out and pick her up when she's able." Bolt took off his boots and socks.

He answered Loretta's questions about the shootings in Etinger while he removed his gunbelt, set it on the table.

Loretta took the shirt for him when he took it off, draped it over a chair to dry.

"Your trousers, too," she said when she turned back around. She thrust her hand out, waiting for him to take them off.

Bolt hesitated a minute, turned his back, unbuttoned his pants and stepped out of them. He handed them back to her without turning around.

Loretta hung the dripping pants over another chair, came back for his shorts.

"Come on. Off with your shorts. They're wet, too."

Bolt turned back to face her.

"You got anything I can wear?"

"Not unless you want one of my nightgowns," she laughed. "I've got a pink gown just like this one." She pulled the front of her robe open to show him.

Bolt couldn't help but notice the full breasts beneath

165

the thin gown, the dark nipples that pushed against the fabric. He glimpsed the dark thatch of her sex just before she drew the robe back around her.

"I think I'll pass," he smiled. "I don't look good in pink."

"I'll tell you what," she laughed. "I'll go in and turn down your bed and you can make a run for it."

Loretta didn't bother to light the lamp in the spare bedroom. The light from the living room spilled over into the bedroom, casting a faint glow across the bed. She pulled the covers back, held them open so he could crawl inside.

Bolt stepped out of the soggy shorts, hung them on a hat rack. He walked to the bedroom, quickly got in bed, pulled the sheet up to his waist.

"Thanks," Bolt said.

She touched his upper arm as if feeling to see if he was feverish.

"Oh, your arm's cold. Are you chilled?"

"No, just damp."

She felt his other arm, his shoulder, his side above the sheet.

"You're cold all over. You could catch pneumonia."

"I'll warm up in a hurry." Loretta's robe had fallen open and Bolt stared boldly at her full breasts beneath the filmy gown.

"I know just the thing to warm you up," she said, ignoring the meaning in his words.

"So do I," Bolt smiled. His eyes drifted down to the Y between her legs. He could see the darkness of her inviting mound that was covered by the thin fabric. He reached a hand out to touch her silky gown, the lovely thigh beneath it.

She side-stepped his advances, pretending that she hadn't felt the brush of his hand.

"Come on now. We've got to get that circulation going again. Roll over on your tummy and let me rub you down."

He moved to the middle of the bed and rolled over, keeping the sheet over his buttocks.

Loretta moved onto the bed, sat with her knees tucked under her.

Her scent drifted up to his nostrils, made him feel giddy.

Working on one shoulder at a time, she rubbed the flesh briskly until it was warm. Bolt felt the tension flow from his body as she massaged his aching muscles with the palms of her hands. He hadn't realized how tired he was until then. He had been in the saddle since dawn and most of it had been hard riding, filled with frustration and fear.

Her touch was firm as her fingers and palms manipulated his flesh. The pressure penetrated deep into the places where he was sore from riding too long. He relaxed as her hands kneaded the flesh of his shoulder blades, rocked down the length of his spine.

She threw the sheet back, exposing his bare bottom. She touched one cheek.

"Even your butt is cold," she said. "You must have been out in that rain a long time."

"Long enough."

She planted both hands on his buttocks, began to massage the fleshy cheeks in a circular motion.

Bolt tensed immediately, from instinct more than anything else.

"Relax," she said. "Your muscles are so hard I can't

even massage them."

He managed to relax the muscles that were clamped tight together. She continued to massage him there with deft fingers. Her touch felt good, the warmth of her hand against the cool dampness of his flesh sending a sensation of pleasure through his nerves. There was something sensuous about her massaging that part of his body. It was such a private place. The warmth flooded through to his loins and he felt his manhood begin to grow as blood engorged it, caused it to thicken.

"Now roll over on your back," she ordered. "I'll warm up your front."

Bolt's cock throbbed when he thought about her warm hands at his loins, rubbing him until he tingled.

When he rolled over, his cock was already fully hard. It jutted out from between his legs, brushed against her hand as he moved.

He grabbed her, drew her soft body to his. Kissed her full on the lips.

"I'm already so hot I'm about to boil over," he husked. "Now let me warm you up."

Chapter Seventeen

Startled by his sudden kiss, she stiffened for an instant, started to free herself from his clutching hands, tried to tear her lips away from his passion. The hard wet pressure of his lips crushing against hers snapped her back to reality, made her realize that the kiss was real. As real as the hot flash of desire that shot through her loins. The ache. The need to be fulfilled. Feelings that were tangible as he flicked his rigid tongue inside the dampness of her mouth. Feelings that she had denied herself for all those years.

She shouldn't have been surprised by his passionate kiss. That was what she wanted, what she had hoped for when she rubbed his bare flesh.

It was happening so fast, she wasn't sure she was ready to give herself, once more, to a man. What if he turned out to be like the others. Cruel and mean and rough. Thinking only of their own pleasure.

When she massaged his back, she had wondered what it would be like to have a man again. She had imagined how it would feel to be probed by a swollen, rigid shaft, how it would feel to have him touch her there where she pulsed. She wanted to know the pleasure as he slipped deep inside her hungry sex cleft where she felt herself dampening.

She knew when she rubbed his back, his bare buttocks, that she wanted him to penetrate, to fill her up with his massive organ. But it was a fantasy and she hadn't realized that she had aroused him to such an extent. Maybe, at least subconsciously, she had massaged his bare flesh for the sole purpose of stimulating him so that he would force her to submit to his advances.

For too many years, she had backed away from men's advances before they got to be anything more than mild flirtations. She had kept a reserve about her, not letting a man get close enough to excite her to the point of no return. Like Tom Penrod. That poor fellow had done everything he could to start something between them that would end up in bed. She had considered it, a couple of times, because she liked Tom. But she had managed to keep herself aloof, stop his advances before he got started. She told herself that he had Tess and didn't need her. If he had been unattached, it might have been a different story. Bolt was attached too, in a way, but Bolt was here and Amylou was not.

She was afraid to relax and let her true feelings be exposed for fear of being hurt again as she had been so many times before. She knew in her mind that all men were not cruel and brutal like the men she had known, but every time she wanted to let herself go, she froze up, protecting her own vulnerability, hiding behind a mask of indifference.

That's why she liked Red Harrington so much. The older man was like a father to her and she knew there would be no sexual demands. He was the only man she knew whom she felt comfortable with, and with him she let herself be natural.

When Bolt had turned over on his back, she had glimpsed his bare rigid cock, wanted him very much, but her old fears had shot a warning to her brain. When he

170

kissed her, she froze for an instant, the fears of her memory suddenly becoming real. She was afraid of Bolt because he was a man. She was afraid of herself.

She shuddered when she thought of her husband, the cruelty of the other men.

Bolt took her quivering body to mean that she was ready for him. He pulled her closer, reached down and found the bare flesh of her legs. He ran his hand under her thin gown, sought the thatch between her legs.

When he touched the damp slit of her sex, she flinched as if struck by a bolt of lightning. Desire flooded her loins as she gushed with the fluids of passion. She knew it had to be now. Now or never. She fell into his arms, kissed him with all the passion that had been trapped inside her body for all those years.

She ravaged his body with fiery kisses, her writhing body smothering him with its heat. She backed away only long enough to slip out of her robe, tear her nightgown away. The gown fell to the floor in a soft heap, a whisper of the things to follow.

Bolt rolled her over on her back. She spread her legs wide to receive him. He positioned himself above her, lowered his throbbing cock to the portal of her steaming sex. He penetrated her oiled sex lips, thrust deep inside her, was bathed in the steaming warmth of her sheath. She thrust her pussy high in the air to welcome his driving shaft.

His flesh slapped against hers as he pounded into her, thrusting deep and long. She bucked and thrashed beneath him, raked her fingernails across his back. He didn't try to stop or slow down. She was too much a woman. He drove his cock into her soaked pussy, basking in her passion. He rammed her again and again with his pulsing cock, until it was too late. Until he felt his seed bubble and boil. Until his heart pounded in his chest. Until his breath came in short gasps.

He plunged deep inside her, let it happen. His milky seed bubbled over, spurted into the folds of her sex as he clutched her tight. He stayed deep inside her until he was drained of everything he had. When he was empty of energy, numb with gratification, he rolled off of her soft body, snuggled in next to her. It was a long time before either one of them spoke.

"You never talk much about your past, do you?" he said, wondering how she could have seemed so cold and unfeeling before and yet so passionate in bed. He knew it had something to do with her past. She had carried the scars of some unpleasant memory far too long.

"No," she said quietly.

"Amylou said you had a bad marriage."

"The worst."

"Would it help to talk about it?"

"It might, but you've helped a lot." She took a breath and then the words tumbled out of her, exorcising her forever. "I married when I was very young, only fifteen years old. I loved my husband very much, or thought I did. But I was too innocent and starry-eyed to know what he was really like. He turned out to be a real bastard. He only wanted me for the sex. Other than that, he didn't pay any attention to me unless he beat me. He drank too much and when he was drunk, he got violent. He spent every nickel he earned as a cowhand on whiskey and women. He got to where he was drinking more than he was working and he got fired, couldn't get another job for more than a day or two. When we ran out of money, he really got brutal with me. I used to have bruises all over me."

"The scars still show, you know," Bolt said. "Not on the surface, but in your eyes."

"I know. I've been so afraid . . . afraid of all men. Until now."

"You can't judge all men by your husband. Most men are decent and good with a woman."

"I didn't, really. It was all those other men. They were all the same way he was. Mean and cruel to me."

"Oh?" Bolt said, surprised to hear her say there had been so many other men.

"Yes. You see, when we ran out of money, my husband forced me to sleep with other men, to become a whore, literally, so he could have money for his damned liquor. He kept me prisoner in my own home. He never let me go into town or even have friends of my own. He kept me tied up at the house when he wasn't there. He brought the men to the house and made me go into the bedroom with them while he waited in the living room until we were finished so he could collect his drinking money. He brought a different man every night, sometimes more than one. He charged them whatever they could give him and most of the time it wasn't much because they were drunkards like he was. They were his drinking companions and they were all just as mean as he was. My husband didn't care if the men assaulted me or not, just so he got his money.

"I'm sorry, Loretta." He drew her in close, tucked her under his arm.

"I was finally able to escape from him, and I came here to this house. The house belonged to my parents when they were alive and I knew my husband didn't know where it was because they moved here after I was married and I never told him about it. But it's been a struggle. I didn't have any money at all and Amylou let me work for her. But she doesn't make much money on the saloon and I haven't been able to save anything. I guess now that she's been robbed, she won't be able to make her payroll, so I won't get anything. But I won't worry about it. I've been through rougher times than this."

"You know what is sad?" Bolt said. "Not that you were so badly treated by your husband and the other men. We all have trials in our life that we must go through. That's what shows us right from wrong, bad from evil. That's how we develop into better people. No, the sad part is that the one experience has soured you on life, on men, and has kept you from enjoying that life and all its pleasures."

"Hey, you sound like a preacher's kid," she smiled, wiping away the tears that had come with her revelation.

"I am," he laughed, squeezing her tight.

They fell asleep in each other's arms, both better because of their talk.

Bolt awoke long before dawn. He planned to leave without waking Loretta up from her peaceful sleep. But he was glad that she got up when he did. He had a couple of questions he wanted to ask, things he had thought about during his fitful sleep.

"Was Sheriff Connors hanging around the saloon last night, around the time of the shooting?" he asked.

"No," she laughed. "That drunken fool wouldn't come in the Red River to spit on the floor. He does all his drinking somewhere else, and plenty of it, I might add. Why?"

"I think that bastard is in on the robbery, somehow. I can't put my finger on it yet, but I think Connors is as

174

crooked as a pig's tail. And my hunches are seldom wrong."

"I've heard that the sheriff has been asking about Tom Penrod, but he hasn't been in the saloon. I don't like him any better than you do, but I think it's just his swaggering personality. His two deputies seem to be decent types. In fact the youngest deputy, Virgil Thorp, came into the saloon for a while last night."

"He did?" Bolt's eyebrows shot up with suspicion.

"Yes, but there's nothing odd about that. He comes in every three or four days to say hello. He's not stuck up like his boss."

"Was Thorp there during the shooting," Bolt asked, knowing he was on the verge of something. A missing piece to the puzzle.

"No, he left about a half hour before the first shots were fired."

"I'll bet Thorp hung around until Tom went upstairs with Tess," Bolt said, seeing the puzzle coming together.

"As a matter of fact, he did. I had just started to sing when I noticed Tom and Tess get up from their table and go upstairs. Thorp left shortly after that, about fifteen minutes. I was beginning to feel rejected," she laughed. "But Thorp's as honest as they come. He wasn't in on the robbery, if that's what you're thinking."

"Unless he was a pawn," Bolt said, thinking out loud. "If Connors ordered him to report to Jake Putnam when Tom went to bed, then he would have followed those orders, not necessarily knowing what it was about.

"I see what you mean . . ."

"Listen, I've got to find Tom. But if I can't find him right away, I want to talk to Tess. Is she at the Red River Saloon?"

"No. She was too frightened to stay there. She's hiding out in an adobe shack on the other side of Houston. I'm the only one who knows where she is, so I knew she'd be safe there."

"Thanks, Loretta. For everything."

Before he left the house, he left a hundred-dollar bill on the table. It was one that he had carried for more than two years, folded and fastened to the inside of his gun-belt, held in place by horse-hair thread. She needed the money and for all the information she had given him, it was well worth the price.

In return for the money, he filled a pocket with a handful of sulfur matches. They just might come in handy where he was going.

The rain had stopped, but it was still pitch black outside when Bolt found the abandoned adobe shack that Loretta had described. It had taken him more than an hour because he had skirted around Houston instead of going through it. It had been easy to find, even though there was no light glowing from the shack. Loretta's directions had been perfect.

He rode up slow and easy, looking for her horse. But it was too dark to see if there was a barn or stable out back.

As he rode up to the adobe house, a familiar odor attacked his nostrils. He breathed in deeply, smelled the scent of a stale, burned-out wood fire. Odd, he thought. It had been warm enough last night that she wouldn't have needed a fire. And yet the smell was there.

He thought about it for a minute, then realized that if she had been caught out in the rain, she might have had to light a fire inside the adobe to dry her clothes. A woman's heavy, long-skirted dress would take a lot more drying than a shirt and a pair of trousers. A wood fire would have made it faster.

He climbed down out of the saddle, pulled a match from his pocket, struck it across his dry trousers. From its small light, he was able to spot a scrub pine. He walked Nick over to the small tree, looped the reins around one of its limbs, after he'd blown the match out, dropped it to the ground.

A horse nickered in the distance as it got wind of Bolt's horse.

Bolt stood perfectly still, listening with keen ears. He didn't hear anything and the horse didn't nicker again. He was sure it was Tess' horse who had whinnied from the back yard.

He picked his way through the darkness until he saw the outline of the adobe in front of him. He felt along the outside wall until he came to a window. There, he stopped and listened. He heard no sounds from inside the house. But the walls were thick and if she was a quiet sleeper, he would not hear her breathing.

He made his way around to the front door, tested the handle. It was unlocked. If the adobe was as old as Loretta had indicated, it was possible that the lock was broken or there was no lock at all. Tess would not need to lock a door anyway, way out here.

He opened the door cautiously, quietly. He stopped to listen again and when he heard no noise, he pushed the door open with his foot. He stepped inside.

He struck another sulfur match, held it high. Its small flame did not give much light, but it was enough for him to see a table in the middle of the room. He moved the match around, trying to see the rest of the room. The flame burned his finger. He dropped it, struck another one. He took a few steps forward, held the match up, saw more of the room.

Just as the second match burned down to his finger, his foot bumped into something on the floor. He threw the match to the ground quickly, fished a third one from his pocket.

He held the match closer to the floor to see what he'd run into. It was a chair. Tipped over on its side.

And then he saw something else.

Tess' high-button shoes, her slim ankles, the hem of her long dress!

Bolt cursed as the flame went out. He whipped out still another one, lit it quickly. He walked alongside her body. That's when he saw it!

Her upper body, her face. And in between, her throat slashed open like a ripe watermelon!

He gasped, nearly gagged at the sight.

He lit another match when that one burned down, looked at the fatal wound. Red blood covered the gaping slash, had dripped down her neck. Beneath her throat was a large stain where the blood had formed a circle, soaked into the dirt floor. He moved the match to look at her face. It was peaceful as if she were sleeping, except for her mouth. That hung open in a dead silent scream.

Suddenly, Bolt heard a sound. It came from behind him.

He hesitated, then reached for his gun.

His hesitation was an instant too long.

A gunbarrel crashed into the back of his skull.

His head swam in a black fog as he pitched forward.

He struggled to remain alert, awake, conscious.

Just before his brain went completely black, he thought he heard his name called.

Chapter Eighteen

"Bolt! Bolt! You all right?"

The voice drifted in and out of Bolt's mind like a wave washing in to shore, then going back out to sea.

A few minutes after he was slammed in the back of the head by a forceful blow with a gunbarrel, Bolt's mind began to clear.

From some dark recess of his brain where there was no space or time, he heard his name being called. Soft at first, then louder, closer. He felt the tap at his cheeks, but it was as if it was someone else's face that was being slapped. He felt the shaking of his shoulders, but that too, seemed to be happening to another body other than his own.

His eyes fluttered open. The room was bathed in a soft glow from a lantern that had been lit while he was unconcious. He blinked his eyes, saw the face of his friend, Tom Penrod, above him. Bolt tried to think where he was. Fragments of horror images floated through his mind. Perhaps he had been dreaming the bad dreams and everything was all right.

"Jeeez, Bolt, I'm sorry. I didn't know it was you," Tom said, hovering above him.

Bolt started to sit up, still not clear about where he was. Pain stabbed at the back of his head when he moved. He reached back, felt the lump on his skull, winced when he touched it.

And then he remembered! Everything! He glanced to his left, saw the lifeless body of Tess Hummer, the grotesque slash across her throat.

"God!" Bolt said as he stood up. "What happened?"

"I don't know." Tom looked at Tess, shook his head. He tried to quell the anger that flared through his mind, the sadness he felt at the loss of a good friend. "Poor Tess. She had nothing to do with any of this and yet she died this way. I tried to find her after the shooting at the Red River Saloon, but I couldn't."

"I heard about the shooting."

"I went to her house in town, but she wasn't there. Neither was her horse. I tracked her here. I found her this . . . this way, about a half an hour before you got here. I waited out back to see if anyone would show up to check on her death. When I heard you ride up, I waited until you got inside, then I came in, figuring to catch her murderer red-handed. I'm sorry if I hurt you, but I thought . . ."

"Forget it, Tom. I've had worse bumps than that. I'm lucky you didn't blow my damn head off."

"You are at that."

"Did you look around for any clues? Any signs of who might have done it?"

"No. I couldn't bear to be in the same room, with her like that . . ."

"I understand. Let's look around." Bolt reached over and felt Tess' dress. It was perfectly dry. Evidently, she had arrived at the adobe shack before the rain hit. "Tom, did you smell anything strange in here?"

Tom sniffed the air.

"Just a hint of wood smoke, now that you mention it."

"I don't think Tess built a fire, do you? I mean, he

180

clothes aren't wet and it was a warm evening, at least not cold enough for a fire. Let's have a look at the fireplace."

Bolt walked over to the table in the middle of the room, started to reach for the lantern that was there, the one that Tom had lit while Bolt was unconscious.

Something else caught his eye and he placed the lamp back down.

"Tom, look at this writing tablet and pencil. It looks like Tess was writing something when she was killed. The chair is tipped over and the position of her body shows that she was probably sitting at the table, right here."

Tom stepped up to the table, glanced at the tablet and pencil.

"Well, if she was writing a note, it sure as hell ain't there now."

"The fireplace! The smell of smoke in here. Whoever killed her must not have liked what she was writing."

The two men carried the lantern to the other side of the room, looked in the firelace. Bolt examined the ashes carefully, saw that papers had been shredded and burned. A piece of charred wood rested near the remains of the burned paper. Bolt held the lamp closer to the ashes, but could not make out any other details.

He carried the lantern back to the table, set it down. He picked up the writing tablet, held it at just the right angle so that he could see an impression on the paper. The murderer had burned the sheet of paper she was writing on, but not the one underneath it. Tess had pressed hard enough with the pencil to leave the marks of her words on the paper below it. If he could only bring those impressions to life, he could tell what she had written. He held the tablet at various angles under the lamp glow, but he was not able to distinguish any particular letters

181

or words.

He set the tablet back on the table, picked up the pencil. It just might work. With an extremely light touch, he traced the pencil across the top part of the paper, moved it back and forth several times, keeping the pressure very light.

It was working! At least some of the impressions were embedded deep enough in the paper to escape the stroke of the pencil when Bolt ran it across. The letters showed up white beneath the dark pencil tracings.

"It's working!" he exclaimed.

Tom hunched over Bolt's shoulder, began to read what was appearing on the blank page.

"Dear Tom . . . hope you . . . safe," read Tom from the words he could make out. ". . . riff Connors . . . I am afraid . . . Conno . . . He want . . . to . . . force Amy . . ."

Bolt continued to trace with the pencil, moving down the page as Tom read aloud the words he could figure out.

". . . out of Red Riv . . . S . . . loon . . . Connors had . . . partner."

"I figured Connors was involved," said Bolt. "The dirty bastard."

". . . Connors' partner . . . works for . . . Amylou. His name . . . is . . . C . . ."

There was just the beginning of the first name of Connors' partner. From the C on the page, there was a straight line going down the page, as if she had slumped over forward as she was writing the name. It was obvious that the murderer had entered and found her at the table, writing the note. It was also obvious that whoever it was, he wanted to destroy the message of the note.

"Well, we figured it was one of Amylou's employees who set us up and now we know for sure."

"But we still don't know who it is, do we?" asked Tom.
"We know it isn't Loretta Sweeney, though."

"I already figured that out," said Bolt.

"But the C could stand for either Carl Anders or Cole Megan."

"And I'm pretty sure I know which one it is," said Bolt. "Now we have to find out who killed Tess."

The first rays of morning light filtered through the dust and grime of the broken windows as Tom and Bolt searched the adobe to see if they could find anything that could help them learn who the killer was. There were no clues inside the house.

When it was light enough, they went outside and checked for a sign. Bolt found what he was looking for after he checked in several places.

"The horse that brought Tess's killer has worn front shoes," said Bolt, pointing to the tracks. "The horse is slightly pigeon-toed. See how the inside curve of both shoes has been worn more there, but make a deeper impression in the damp ground?"

"I see it," said Tom. "Wonder who the horse belongs to. I've got a little debt to settle. For Tess. Let's ride to Houston."

"What about Tess?" Bolt asked. "Do you want to take her back to town for burial?"

"No. I think I'll leave her here. I'll come back out and bury her out here where it's peaceful, away from the corruption of the city."

Bolt heard the bitterness in Tom's voice. He knew what Tom would do when he found the man who killed his sweetheart.

It was ten in the morning when Tom and Bolt rode into

Houston. Bolt had a couple of people he wanted to see, but he wanted to put his horse in the stable first, ask the stable boy a couple of questions.

"Let's drop our gear off at the Sundowners before we go to the livery," Bolt said. "No need to lug it around."

They rode in the back way to Houston, stayed off the main street completely. They came in behind the Sundowners Hotel, used the back entrance to carry in Bolt's saddlebags and bedroll.

They lugged the heavy gear upstairs, walked toward Bolt's room. As he stepped up to the door of his room, he thought he heard a noise inside. He paused to listen, figured the noise had come from someplace else. Nevertheless, to be on the safe side, he set the saddlebags on the floor, slipped his pistol out of its holster, opened the door cautiously. He didn't see anyone at first, so he kicked the door wider, stepped inside, his pistol ready.

"Bolt!" called the voice in the room.

Bolt froze, his heart skipped a beat.

"Bolt! I'm so glad you're safe!" Amylou limped over to Bolt, threw her arms around him.

"Well, Amylou! And Connie. I'm glad you're here."

"Connie brought me in on her buckboard. I had to find out how you were and where you were. I didn't know where else to look. I knew you'd come back here if . . ."

"Good to see you both. Thanks, Connie. For bringing her to town."

"Think nothing of it," said Connie Gaines. "I was heading this way anyway. I decided I didn't want to live in Etinger any longer."

"Tom, this is Constance Gaines. She took care of Amylou when she was hurt."

"Pleased ta meet you," Tom mumbled.

184

"Amylou, Tess was killed. We found her this morning," Bolt said.

"Oh, no!" She looked over at Tom. "I'm sorry, Tom."

"Listen," said Bolt. "Will you girls wait right here? We're going to take our horses over to the stables."

"Will you be right back?" Amylou asked.

"Not right back. We have a couple of calls to make."

"Bolt, no. You're still looking for Bascomb, aren't you?"

"Among others, yes."

"Can't you let it go, Bolt?" begged Amylou. Enough people have died already. I don't care about the money anymore. I'm so afraid that you'll get . . ." She couldn't bring herself to say the word.

"You know I have to do it," Bolt said. "No matter how it comes out."

"I know. Be careful. Please." She kissed him on the cheek, hoped it wouldn't be the last kiss.

"I'm always careful," he grinned.

At the stable, Bolt asked Ronnie Hall to take care of Nick and Tom's horse.

"I always take good care of 'ol Nick," the freckle-faced lad said. He led the horses into separate stalls where there were buckets of water. He would grain them and groom them right away.

"I know you do, Ronnie." Bolt took out a five-dollar bill, gave it to the boy. "They've had some rough riding the past couple of days."

"I've wondered about you, but I knew you'd be O.K. Did you catch the robbers?"

"Some of them."

"Sheriff Connors has been in here looking for your

horse, askin' if you were back yet. Said he was gonna send a posse out to help you track the robbers if you weren't back by today. He'll be glad to know you're back.''

"I'm sure he will be," Bolt said, trying to keep the sarcasm from being obvious. "Say, Ronnie, do you know of any horses that are pigeon-toed?"

"Sure. Sheriff Connors has a horse that's pigeon-toed. It's a piebald roan. Good horse, but knock-kneed as hell. Why'd you ask?"

Bolt and Tom looked at each other.

They knew now who Tess's killer was.

Sheriff Connors!

Bolt saw the anger creep into Tom's face, saw him pat the butt of his pistol.

"Just curious, Ronnie."

"Well, you stop by and tell the sheriff you're back in town. I'm sure he'll want to make a full report. That's what he said, anyway."

"Thanks, Ronnie. We'll take care of the sheriff."

"We certainly will," said Tom, a fierce hatred in his heart.

Outside the stable, Bolt looked at his friend, saw his face turn red with anger.

"That dirty son of a bitch!" Tom cried.

"Tom, get a hold on yourself. Don't let your anger and hatred control you."

"I'm going to kill that filthy bastard!"

"I know you are, but you've got to calm down. You walk in there like you are now and you're likely to make a costly mistake. Now settle down."

Tom kicked his toe into the dirt. He wanted to lash out. He wanted to kill.

"It's mighty hard to do," he said, "but I know you're

186

right." He took a deep breath. "I'm ready whenever you are."

"I'm ready, too," said Bolt as he made a final check of his pistol, the extra ammunition in his gunbelt.

They marched a short block to the sheriff's office, checked their weapons once more before opening the door.

Deputy Virgil Thorp looked up from the desk, smiled.

"Howdy, gentlemen. Glad you're back. Did you catch the . . ."

"Never mind that," said Bolt. "Is Connors here?"

"Yes, he's here, but he's busy in the back room." Thorp nodded his head in the direction of the room. "You'll have to wait until he's finished."

"The hell we will!" said Bolt, starting for the door to the room.

"No! You can't go in there. The sheriff said he wasn't to be disturbed. Besides, the door's locked."

Bolt slid his hand over so it rested on the butt of his pistol.

Just before he crashed through the door.

Chapter Nineteen

Bolt whipped his pistol out as he broke down the door. Tom was right behind him, his pistol already drawn.

They caught the sheriff by surprise.

Connors wasn't alone.

The two men sat across from each other at a table in the middle of the room. In between them sat the empty cloth money sacks that once belonged to Amylou.

Bascomb's left hand contained a wad of bills, the other hand a single bill. His hand was half way across the table as he counted out the money, splitting it with the sheriff.

"What the hell . . . !" yelled Connors. His hand started for his gun as his mouth fell open in surprise.

"Don't try it, Connors," Bolt warned.

Bascomb dropped the money in his hand, went for his gun.

Tom stepped up quickly.

"No, you don't!" Tom shouted.

Both the men put their hands on the table.

"You bastards have got some answerin' to do, so you'd better spit it out while you still got the breath to talk," Bolt said.

"I don't know what you're talking about," Connors said. "This is private business and you're not invited."

Tom moved around behind Bolt, trained his pistol at the sheriff's head.

"You're gonna talk, Connors," he said. "Then you're

gonna die!"

Bolt glanced at the even stacks of money on both sides of the table. He looked at Bascomb, aimed his gun at his head.

"So, you split your money half and half," said Bolt. "Why do you split with the sheriff. He never did anything for you?"

"You'll never get away with this," Bascomb said, his eyes leveled at Bolt. "If you kill me, I've trained a man to take my place. He'll stalk you, find you when you least expect it. You're as good as dead now, Bolt."

"You talkin' about Leacock?"

"Yeah, I'm talkin' about Leacock. The best there is. He'll drop you before you know he's there."

"Hell, Leacock walked out on you back at Eagle Lake. You've got nothing left, Bascomb. Face it. You're going to hang for all your crimes, for all the murders you've committed. But don't count on a fair trial. They'll lynch you first."

Bascomb glared at Bolt, wanted to take him out.

Bolt wanted him to go for it. He wanted an excuse to kill him on the spot.

"You got a pigeon-toed roan?" Tom asked the sheriff.

"None of your business," snapped Connors.

"I've made it my business," said Tom. "You killed Tess, didn't you?"

The sheriff's eyes widened in surprise. He knew he'd been caught. There was no way out of the mess now, except to shoot his way out. If he could just stall long enough, he'd distract them, shoot them both when they weren't looking.

He slowly pushed away from the table, kept his hands high so they wouldn't fire, stood up. He stood with his

189

feet apart, his barrel chest puffed out.

"Listen, boys. There's been some misunderstanding. I've just arrested Bascomb for you. He was just counting out the money so I could return it to its proper owners. That being you, Bolt, and Miss Amylou Lovett." Connors eased his hands down to his waistline, tucked his thumbs inside the waistband. He made it look too casual.

Bolt watched his hands very carefully, expecting him to draw at any minute. Tom watched him, too.

"Bullshit," said Bolt.

"Now you boys just take the money and leave. I'm very busy, as you can see."

"You killed Tess!" Tom said again. "You'd better draw your weapon 'cause I'm gonna blow your head off either way." Tom cocked his pistol, curled his finger around the trigger. He aimed the pistol between Connors' eyes, started to squeeze the trigger.

Connors saw it coming. He had only one chance to win.

"Yes! I killed Tess," he shouted. "She knew too much!" He went for it. His hand shot to his pistol butt, whipped it out.

Tom shot him before he could squeeze the trigger.

Right between the eyes.

Connors gasped as the bullet made a neat hole right between his eyes. The back of his head blew apart as the bullet exploded. His eyes glazed over in death. He stumbled backwards, reeled against the wall. He slid slowly down the wall, dead before he pitched over forward and slammed against the floor.

Bascomb stared at the sheriff's body, saw the hole in his forehead, the blood that started to trickle from the clean bullet wound. He could not take his eyes off the stark horror.

"Your turn's next," said Bolt. "You either tell us who your partner is or you buy it here and now. You want to live long enough to hang, you name names."

"Connors is . . . was my partner."

"I'm not talking about that partner, Bascomb, and you know damned well I'm not. Which one of Amylou's employees is your partner? Who set us up for the robbery?" Bolt glared at the tall man with cold blue eyes.

Suddenly, Bascomb pushed away from the table. His chair tumbled over backwards. His hand was a blur as it shot to his holster.

Bolt took aim, started to squeeze the trigger. He waited until Bascomb hammered back before he pulled the trigger.

The bullet hit Bascomb just where Bolt wanted it to. A lung shot. Fatal, but not instant death.

Bascomb's body jerked back as he took the impact of the bullet. He clutched at his chest, drew back bloody hands. He tried to keep his balance, but stumbled backwards, then fell to the floor.

Foamy pink spittle bubbled from his mouth as he tried to curse.

Bolt stepped over to him, aimed the pistol at his head.

Bascomb's hand still gripped his pistol. It was cocked, ready to shoot. He started to raise it slow so Bolt wouldn't see.

Bolt slammed his boot down on Bascomb's wrist, heard the bones snap. The pistol tumbled out of Bascomb's hand. Bolt kicked it away.

Blood poured out of the hole in his chest. It stained a wide red circle on his shirt, dripped to the floor where it formed a puddle.

"You're gonna die, Bascomb, a slow, painful death.

You're going to choke and gag and fight for every breath. You only got one chance to make things right before you go. Who set us up for the robbery? Which one of Amylou's help?"

Bascomb opened his mouth to speak, choked on blood. He struggled to get a breath.

"It . . . it . . . was . . . C—C . . ."

His eyes fell open in a vacant stare. His mouth gaped open in a grotesque smile. He died before he could answer their question.

Bolt heard the noise behind him. He whirled around, faced the broken door, his pistol ready.

Deputy Thorp stepped inside the room, looked at the dead bodies.

"You gonna take us on?" Bolt asked.

Thorp's hands shot up in the air, chest high.

"No, sir. They both got what they deserved. I'm sorry about last night, Penrod."

"For what?" Tom asked.

"I was the one who told Jake Putnam you had gone up to bed. Connors told me they was going to play a practical joke on you. I swear, I didn't know Connors was crooked until after the shooting."

"That's all right, Thorp," Tom said. "Now that Connors is gone, this town is going to need a new sheriff. Maybe you can bring some honest law to this community."

Tom walked over to the table and helped Bolt gather up the money, stuff it into the cloth bags. When they were through, Bolt tucked the bags inside his shirt, buttoned his shirt back up.

"Well, that about winds it up," said Tom as they left the sheriff's office.

"Not quite," Bolt told him. "We still got one man to face down."

"Yair, let's go get it over with."

"A good idea, Tom. I'm about ready to hit the trail again when this is over with. How about you?"

"Yeah. I don't much feel like stickin' around here, now that Tess is gone."

They both reloaded their pistols, went straight from the sheriff's office to the Red River Saloon.

They opened the door and went inside.

Bolt was surprised to see Amylou and Connie there.

Amylou hobbled up to Bolt, hugged him.

"Oh, I was so worried about you," she said.

"What are you doing here?"

"I figured you still wanted to talk to my employees, so I've got them all here waiting for you."

Loretta walked up behind Amylou, smiled at Bolt and Tom.

"I'm glad you're both back safe and sound," she said quietly. "Amylou told me about Tess. I'm sorry, Tom."

"Me too," he mumbled.

Bolt glanced around the room. He saw Carl Anders slouched down in a chair by a back table, a sullen look on his face. Cole Megan leaned against the back wall, talking to Anders, telling the bartender how unfair it was for Amylou to call them in on their free time.

Carl agreed, said that Amylou should pay them for their time.

"Come on, Amylou. Let's go on back to the table," Bolt said.

Tom stepped in close to Bolt, spoke in a low voice. He glanced in the direction of the back table.

"You know, Bolt, I just thought about something.

193

Maybe both Cole and Carl are in on it. You may have more trouble than you bargained for."

"Tom, don't go looking for trouble," Bolt said. "We got enough as it is."

"Just thought I'd keep you on your toes," Tom smiled.

But Bolt was sure he knew which man was involved with Connors and Bascomb. He could see it in his eyes. Bolt was pretty confident that the employee didn't know that Bolt still suspected him of his part in the scheme. It would be interesting to see his reaction.

"Amylou," he whispered, "stay to my left when we get to the table. I don't want you getting hurt if anything happens."

Tom walked ahead of Bolt and Amylou, Loretta behind them. He stopped at the back table, stepped aside to let Bolt and Amylou get closer.

"Thanks for coming, folks," Bolt said, looking at the two men. "It was important or I wouldn't have asked." He looked at Amylou, hoped she didn't mind him taking the credit for arranging the meeting.

"Get on with it," grumbled Carl Anders. "This here's my own time. You want ta talk to us, it's the same as working. If we have to be here, we get paid."

"Yeah," said Cole Megan. "You was told not to butt into business that wasn't your own."

"You still accusing us of conspiracy, or whatever the hell it is?" Anders said sarcastically.

"I'm not accusing anyone," Bolt said calmly. "I just want to get to the facts."

"You've got a lot of nerve coming here demanding to talk to us," said Cole. "You're nothing but a pimp, an owner of whorehouses. What gives you the right to question us?"

"For your information, Mr. Megan, I am not a pimp. I've never sold a woman in my life. Fact is, I've made the lot of the soiled doves a little better. I don't tell 'em what to do. They pick their life and if they work for me, they get paid."

"It's wrong," said Megan.

"Nothing wrong with servicing a man for pay. If that's your talent. But I don't fix them up or train them. I just give them a place to sleep and they split their earnings with me. Call it rent. I'm a landlord."

"You make yourself sound real pure and innocent, don't you, Bolt?" taunted Megan.

"I've got my faults, Megan. Just like you and Carl and all the rest of us. But pimping ain't one of 'em."

"One of your faults," said Carl Anders, "is you bringing us in here this early in the morning. A man's got to get his sleep if he's expected to work the night shift."

"Yeah," agreed Megan. "You waste our time, questioning us like some sheriff and accusing us of things that ain't true."

"I told you I'm not accusing you," Bolt said, almost enjoying the grumbling of the men, their reaction to his presence. "Besides, I didn't come here to question you. I came to bring good news. For all of you." He paused, waited to see their reaction.

"I'll bet," said Anders.

Bolt reached inside his shirt, drew out the three small cloth bags. He purposely placed them on the table, within easy reach of either Megan or Anders.

"Amylou, I've recovered your money."

"Oh, that's great," squealed Amylou.

Bolt watched Megan's face carefully. He saw the man's eyes go cold, his lips clamp tight together. Anders, on the other hand, looked pleased at the news of the recovered money.

"This is good news for all of you, as I said." Bolt played it for all it was worth, trying to make Megan crack. "This means Amylou can meet her payroll today. All of you will get paid. Of course, one paycheck doesn't amount to nearly as much as all this money put together." He opened the bags, dumped the paper bills on the table. He saw Megan turn a little green around the gills.

"How'd you get it back?" Amylou asked, playing right into Bolt's hands without knowing it.

"Took some doing. We had to kill Sheriff Connors and Bascomb to get it. When Bascomb knew he was dying, he told me that all of this money was to go to his silent partner. I'll bet that partner is going to be mighty sick when he finds out how much money he missed."

Megan couldn't stand it anymore. He stepped up to the table, started to grab the money.

"Back off, Megan," Bolt said, his hand hovering above his pistol. "It's not your money. You didn't do anything to deserve it. Of course, out of all that money, you'll get your paycheck."

"I've been cheated!" he screamed. "A third of that was to go to me! Bascomb planned to cut his other men out of their split. He was going to fire them anyway, said they hadn't earned anything because they couldn't kill you, Bolt. It's mine! And you're not going to stop me from taking it!" He whipped out his pistol, cocked it on the upswing. He aimed it right at Bolt.

Chapter Twenty

Bolt fired before Megan could get off his shot. Bolt aimed for Megan's shooting hand, hit it with one shot. Everyone there heard the bone-crunching shot as it tore into Megan's hand.

Megan screamed in pain as the pistol fell from his hand, dropped to the floor.

Tom stepped in, kicked the gun away from the table, then walked over and picked it up.

"I could kill you, Megan," Bolt said, "but I'm going to let you live. You'll have a crippled hand the rest of your life. Maybe it'll remind you of what happened because of your greed. Of course, you'll never be able to deal cards again. Or use a gun or a knife unless you start practicing with your left hand right away."

"You bastard!" Megan yelled. "You dirty, filthy bastard. I'll kill you for this and you won't even know it's coming."

"Not with that hand, you won't," Bolt said. "You know why I'm letting you live? Because I want you to go out and show the world what happens to men like you. You're an example, Megan, an example of greed. I want you to go out and tell all those outlaws that there is justice after all. A man can only push society so far before he backs himself against the wall. Remember that every time you want to shake hands with your ugly hand. In fact, I'll bet the sawbones will have to cut the hand off at the wrist. You won't even have a hand to shake with. You're right-handed, aren't you, Megan? Think about it every time you try to write with a pencil. Think of it when you comb your hair, or take a piss. Think of your greed when you want a woman and she turns away after seeing your ugly stump of a hand."

"Stop! Stop! I can't take it anymore," Megan cried. He put his hands to his ears, to shut out Bolt's words. Except that his right hand didn't make it. It fell limp at the end of his arm.

"See what I mean?" Bolt said sarcastically.

Megan started to make a fist. There was no fist to make. There were no muscles left to control the fingers.

There was only a limp, bloody appendage at the end of his arm, dangling. Useless.

"This calls for a celebration," Amylou said after Megan left to find the doctor. "The drinks are on the house."

"Amylou," Bolt said, "you'll never make any money that way. You've got to start watching your pennies if you're going to make this the biggest, best place in Houston. Takes a lot of money to remodel these days."

"Oh, Bolt, you're impossible," she said, then turned to the boy who worked for her. He had been sweeping when the commotion began. He stood there, still, leaning against his broom, awestruck by Bolt's fast draw. "Charlie, would you bring us a couple of bottles of whiskey and some glasses? Carl's not on duty yet and I'd sure hate to pay him extra." She giggled, looked over at Carl. He smiled, shook his head.

Amylou counted out the money on the table as the others sat down and watched. She stacked it in two neat piles, pushed one toward Bolt.

"Here's your poker winnings, Bolt," she said.

"You keep it, Amylou. You're going to need it if you plan to improve this place."

"Oh, no you don't. That's your money. You won it fair and square. Any money I take, I earn. I don't ever want to be accused of being greedy. I'd hate to lose my hand over that. Hell, I can't even talk without using my hands."

Carl Anders sat up from his slouched position for the first time since he sat down. He leaned forward, looked at Amylou.

"Pardon me, Amylou, but would you think me greedy if I asked for my paycheck now?"

"Of course not, Carl." She handed him what he had earned and a twenty-dollar bonus.

"Now I've got another favor to ask," he smiled.

"What's that, Carl?"

"Could I have the night off? I think I'd like to get good and drunk tonight."

"You've got it, Carl. Just don't make a habit of it," she smiled. She knew he wouldn't. Carl hardly ever drank whiskey. He'd probably be sick as a dog tomorrow. "Take two days off, Carl. You may need it."

"With pay?" he smiled.

"You drive a hard bargain. Yes, with pay."

Charlie set the bottles and glasses on the table.

"Come on and sit down, Charlie," Bolt said. "I'll buy you a drink."

"I'm not old enough."

"You are today."

Bolt poured whiskey all around, held his glass in the air.

"To the Red River Saloon," he toasted. "May she

199

continue to grow. May she still be standing a hundred years from now."

Glasses clinked together around the table.

Carl Anders polished off his drink in one gulp, excused himself from the table. He was ready to sleep the day away, then get ready for a night of hooting and hollering. He just didn't know where to go to do his drinking. He sure as hell didn't want to do it at the Red River Saloon, but it was the best place in town.

Charlie looked at the glass, wrinkled his nose when he smelled it. He took a deep breath, stuck out his chest, grinned, then took a big drink like he'd seen Carl do. He came up sputtering and coughing as the whiskey burned his throat.

"I think I'll wait a few more years," he grinned sheepishly, then got up and left the table.

The other people at the table drank their drinks, talked about the events of the past two days. They didn't mention the shootings or the deaths, only the good things that happened, the funny things.

Loretta sat next to Tom, looked at him in new light. She was no longer afraid of a good man, and Tom seemed like a hell of a nice guy.

"Oh, Tom, I almost forgot," she said. "I've got something for you."

"What's that?" he asked, trying to figure out what was different about her.

"Just a minute." Loretta dashed into the office, came back out carrying Tom's new Stetson. She handed it to him.

Everyone at the table stared at the number of bullet holes in the hat.

"I found this after the shootout," Loretta explained.

"I thought you'd like to see it."

"Jeeez, look at that," he said, starting to count the bullet holes.

"Seven of them," she said. "I already counted them. That man was packing a pair of six-guns."

"Whose hat is that?" Bolt asked, not recognizing it.

"Mine," smiled Tom as he lifted it to his head.

"Damn good thing you weren't wearing it at the time," smiled Bolt. "Or were you?"

"Looks like you're going to have to get yourself another hat," Loretta said.

Tom took it off, held it in his hand, spun it around on one finger. He thought of Tess when he looked at it.

"I think I'll keep it," Tom said softly. "It's been pretty lucky for me."

"I'd think so," Bolt said.

"Bolt, I've got something to take care of out at the adobe. I'm going to ride out there now."

Bolt knew what he was talking about.

"You want me to go with you?" he offered.

"No, I think I'll do it myself."

"I'll go with you, Tom," Loretta said.

He looked at her, saw the softness in her eyes.

"It's not necessary."

"Tess was my friend, too."

He didn't know how to tell her.

"Amylou, Tom and I have decided it's time to move on," Bolt said simply.

"Move on?" she asked, surprised. "Where are you going?"

"To San Antonio next. From there I don't know."

"You're not going today, are you?"

"No, we'll ride out in the morning."

She lowered her head, fought back the tears. Finally, she looked up at him.

"I'll miss you, Bolt. Will you come back to see me sometime?"

"Want to go with us?" he smiled.

She thought a minute.

"No. My roots are here. I want to make a success of my business. But more important, I want to marry someday and raise children, have a home in the country. All those things girls dream about when they're growing up. Besides," she smiled, "I don't think you're the marrying kind."

"No. Not yet, at least. Maybe someday . . ."

"I understand, Bolt. I guess I knew from the beginning that you wouldn't be here long. But it's been quite an experience. It's been good."

"For me, too."

"Bolt, Connie could go with you. That's where you're headed, isn't it, Connie?"

"Yes. I've heard they need good nurses in San Antonio. I'd planned on leaving in the morning. I brought all my things in my buckboard."

"What made you decide to leave Etinger, Connie?" Bolt asked.

"I just got tired of patching up men who had nothing better to do than shoot each other up. Men on both sides of the law. I want to go where I can do some good, where I can take care of sick children and women who need me. And men who have some regard for another human being's life."

"You're welcome to travel with us if you want to do the cooking. Tom's a terrible cook."

"You've got yourself a deal."

It was late afternoon when Tom and Loretta returned from burying Tess Hummer.

"Guess what, Tom," Bolt said. "We're going to have company on our trip to San Antonio. Connie's going with us, at least that far."

"Great," said Tom. "I hope you can cook. If you can't, you're in for a rough trip. Bolt can't even boil coffee, let alone cook a decent meal."

Connie and Amylou giggled.

"That's just what he said about you," Connie said. "Don't worry, I'm a great cook. And if you get shot by an arrow, I can take care of that, too."

"Hey, Tom, aren't you forgetting something?"

"What's that, Bolt?"

"You know that sock I gave you to keep for me while I was gone?"

"Oh, yes, of course."

"Well, I'd like to have it back if you haven't lost it."

"Lost it? Are you kidding? It never left my sight."

"Well, could I have it?"

"Yair. Just a minute. I'll go get it."

"Where is it?"

"Hidden in a very safe place in my room."

"I thought you never let it out of your sight."

"Well, hardly ever."

Loretta covered her mouth quickly, trying to hide a smile behind her hand. It was all she could do to keep a straight face. She knew the history of that dark blue sock. She also knew what was inside. And Tom still had a surprise coming when he went to look for it.

"Well, could I have it?" Bolt asked.

When Tom went up the stairs, Loretta went into the

203

office, then followed Tom upstairs.

Tom's room was a shambles by the time she got there.

"Shit!" Tom said when she came in. "I can't find that damned sock anywhere. It's not in my rifle sheath where I put it. I've searched through everything."

"Did you look under the mattress?" she asked, stifling a giggle.

"Yes. But I didn't put it there again. I thought maybe you'd change the sheets again and throw it away. God, I can't find it anywhere. What am I going to do? Do you know what's inside that sock?"

"Another smelly sock," she said, managing to keep a straight face. "That's what you told me."

"No. It's Bolt's money. He'll strangle me if I've lost it." Tom removed the rifle from the sheath, shook the sheath for the umpteenth time. He searched through his bedroll, the saddlebags, the drawers of his dresser. "I could have sworn I put it in there with my rifle."

Loretta drew her hand from behind her back, held up the blue sock in front of her.

"This what you're looking for?"

"Oh, thank God," he said, wiping his brow with his hand. "Where'd you find it?"

"I didn't. Tess gave it to me before she rode to the adobe. For safekeeping."

"She was quite a woman."

"That she was."

Tom and Loretta went downstairs laughing. Tom handed the sock to Bolt.

"See, I told you I could take care of it for you. I knew where it was every minute you were gone."

"I'll bet you did, Tom," Bolt smiled. "Sometime, when I've got an extra hour or two, I'd like to hear about it."

204

"Bolt, you don't think I . . ."

"Yes, I do, Tom. You'd lose your own pecker if it wasn't fastened on."

It was sad saying goodbye to Amylou and Loretta, but Bolt and Amylou had spent one last night together. They hadn't done much sleeping, but Bolt didn't care. He had the rest of his life to catch up on his sleep. He knew she'd do well with her saloon because men like Connors and Bascomb were gone from the town, at least until the next breed came along. Cole Megan didn't have to be fired. After he got his hand patched up, he left town of his own accord. He'd never be back and the doctor had told them that Megan would never have use of his hand again. It would always be a limp, dangling reminder of his greed.

Bolt hitched Nick and Connie's horse to the front of the buckboard so that he could ride with her on the buckboard seat. Tom followed behind, riding his own horse.

"What's it like to be a whore?" Connie asked when they were a few miles out of town.

"Honey, if you have to ask, the life isn't for you. Some of them get rich, but most of them just get old. Besides, you've a calling already. You're a damned fine nurse."

"Is that all I'm good for?"

"Well, no, that's not all." He drew her closer on the buckboard seat, kissed her passionately.

Tom watched the couple, didn't see how he could exist during the trip if they were going to sneak off in the bushes at every stop. And the way things were looking, that's what they would do.

"Hey, Bolt, I'm going to ride back to town and talk to Loretta about something."

"Save yourself the trouble," Bolt said. "Loretta

205

charges more than you could afford."

"Her—she—she's a whore?"

"Must be. I spent one night with her and she charged me a hundred bucks."

"But that was for information, wasn't it?"

"Could be."

"Well, I'm going back, anyway. I'll catch up to you in San Antonio in a few days. There's no way I'm going to ride with you two love birds making hay at every rest stop. I'd be a raving maniac by the time we got to San Antonio."

"Too bad, Tom. You might learn something."

Bolt smiled, drew Connie close to him on the buckboard seat. They would have a good trip without Tom around to spoil their fun.

THE GUNN SERIES BY JORY SHERMAN

GUNN #1: DAWN OF REVENGE   (594, $1.95)
Accused of killing his wife, William Gunnison changes his name to Gunn and begins his fight for revenge. He'll kill, maim, turn the west blood red—until he finds the men who murdered his wife.

GUNN #2: MEXICAN SHOWDOWN   (628, $1.95)
When Gunn rode into the town of Cuchillo, he didn't know the rules. But when he walked into Paula's Cantina, he knew he'd learn them.

GUNN #3: DEATH'S HEAD TRAIL   (648, $1.95)
With his hands on his holster and his eyes on the sumptuous Angela Larkin, Gunn goes off hot—on his enemy's trail.

GUNN #4: BLOOD JUSTICE   (670, $1.95)
Gunn is enticed into playing a round with a ruthless gambling scoundrel—and playing around with the scoundrel's estranged wife!

GUNN #8: APACHE ARROWS   (791, $2.25)
Gunn gets more than he bargained for when he rides in with pistols cocked to save a beautiful settler woman from ruthless Apache renegades.

GUNN #9: BOOTHILL BOUNTY   (830, $2.25)
When Gunn receives a desperate plea for help from the sumptuous Trilla, he's quick to respond—because he knows she'll make it worth his while!

GUNN #10: HARD BULLETS   (896, $2.25)
The disappearance of a gunsmith and a wagon full of ammo sparks suspicion in the gunsmith's daughter. She thinks Gunn was involved, and she's up-in-arms!

GUNN #11: TRIAL BY SIXGUN   (918, $2.25)
Gunn offers help to a pistol-whipped gambler and his well-endowed daughter—only to find that he'll have to lay more on the table than his cards!

GUNN #12: THE WIDOW-MAKER   (987, $2.25)
Gunn offers to help the lovely ladies of Luna Creek when the ruthless Widow-maker gang kills off their husbands. It's hard work, but the rewards are mounting!

MORE FANTASTIC READING FROM ZEBRA!